Punk

Lex J. Grootelaar

"I am madness maddened!"
- Moby Dick

CHAPTER 1

I awoke cold on the shoulder of a highway. I had no idea how I got there. As the song goes, I found my mind in a brown paper bag—only this wasn't the sixties, and the bag was clear, not brown. My life felt like a cliché as I found myself in this shoulder—this ditch. I slowly stood up. A semi-truck whirled by sending up a dirt cloud. I choked. To complete the cliché, I held out a thumb: the one that had been broken the year before when I fell out of a bar. The cars flew by and filled the air with exhaust. I smiled beside myself. Beside my life. I smiled at all the self-destruction, the missed opportunities, the lust, and the indulgences... All the indulgences. The thought carried as the wind blew. Finding my sunglasses in the high grass, I put them on hiding my bloodshot eyes and, hopefully, the haggard sketchiness that those eyes contained. As I looked at the empty eyes of drivers passing me on their way to work, my sympathy was with them. What day was this? What month? What year? When did the bender start? When would it finish? Finally, a car slowed as I gazed up at the sun just showing itself.

Running to the car on the shoulder, I attempted to piece together what happened the night before. Did my run-in with the Afeller boys go amiss? Their punk rock band was becoming so big—and with it, lots of new characters were on the scene. Did I offend some white-top? Something about his mother, I'm sure. The car put on its hazards as the driver opened his window and gestured me over. I ran my hands over my patched black jeans. I guess they didn't offend; nor did my red and blond Mohawk that I never wore up.

I opened the door and peered in. The man was fortyish. He looked like a family man in his suit and tie. I smiled, knowing I was everything he wouldn't want his children to become. And yet he offered me a ride.

"Hey there. You from the city, or some drifter?"

"Neither. I'm not from this city, nor a drifter. I'm a man of the land with nothing but my good sense to guide me through waters deep and quick."

"Son, I'm not some girl at the bar, I'm the man driving you back to the city. So save the bullshit. Do you want some coffee? I have a thermos. You must drink coffee?" The man smiled as he passed over a thermos and a small brown disposable cup.

"Thanks. I know you're not a girl at the bar, so I *will* put away my charm—and yes, I drink coffee, but only when I smoke. And I seem to be out," I said as I lazily checked my black leather jacket and found nothing but an empty pack.

"You're a drifter then; smoking's a dying pastime. A losing battle."

"Then you don't partake?"

"Lucky for you, son, I'm also a dying breed." He pulled out a silver case full of long cigarettes.

"Thanks," I said as he passed me the case.

"You have a name? A real name? I offered you my smokes and my coffee; least you can do is give me a name." I lit the cigarette and sipped the coffee.

"A real name, eh?" I took a long drag. "Clark. Clark Kent," I smiled at him.

"Superman, eh? Fully able to fly, but stuck in an '85 Toyota, smoking my cigarettes, drinking my coffee and dressed in a fashion that I take it Lois Lane picked out?"

"Yeah, she's a great dame." I kept trying to remember what had happened last night.

"Humph. Where in the city are you going? Or should I just shoot for the downtown homeless shelter?"

"Mid-city would be good. I just need to get to my bike. It's in a garage I rent with the money I make saving the world and all."

"What were you doing on the side of the road? Good old Lex Luthor leave you high and dry?"

"If you must know, he attacked me with kryptonite and took my cape. I wouldn't need the lift if I had the cape. You should know that."

"Good point. Have some more coffee. A bike guy, eh?"

"Harley guy. It was my father's," I replied.

"A gift for your law school graduation?"

"Stolen."

I could see the city approaching, the skyscrapers visible with an early morning summer haze around them.

"And what do you do for work there, Clark?"

"Me? The usual philanthropy, human projects, building churches, and feeding the poor."

"Ah, a fine job for Superman."

"Fine job for any man. You wouldn't happen to have anything... I could put in this coffee?" I asked.

"I'm a family man myself—but like I said, a dying breed. Look inside the glove compartment."

I opened it, and inside was a small bottle of bourbon. This was a man after my own heart. I poured a healthy amount into my mug.

"And for you?"

"No thanks; not before lunch." As he shoulder-checked, I slipped the bottle into my inside jacket pocket.

"Let me guess," I said. "You were a '60s hippy into the drug scene who got some flower child knocked up and started looking at things seriously. Your college degree wouldn't get you far, so you got into sales. You don't work in the office, hence the road drinks and the engraved cigarette holder: a gift for being with the company maybe fifteen years. You have children in their teens and you wish for nothing more than for them to go to college, get good jobs, and become nothing like you used to be—and definitely nothing like me."

He laughed. "The world is a cruel place and not for the faint. Don't doubt that you're heading down a bad path: one where your super powers won't be enough to save you. One day you'll need redemption, but no one will show you any mercy. You'll cry out, and no one will answer." He stared at me, no longer watching the road. I looked back at him.

"Let me tell you something, man. I've cried out already. I've cried to the world, and you know what the world said back? It said no, just like you're saying it would. But you know why that makes me better than a day driver—a day salesman whose life lost its lustre over the years?" I pulled the bottle out of my jacket and took a long swig, looking at him as I did. "The world has also cried out to me. And I was the one saying no, just the same. I fight the good fight and walk down the road walked by so many others, but I will never falter. I will never cave. I will seek out a life all want, but none have the courage to live."

"Keep the bottle, then, and let your destruction swallow you whole. And if you come out alive, the tie and jacket will welcome you on the other side—and there will be someone like me, bailing you out."

We drove into the city.

"Drop me off by Manulife Place." I was feeling the kind of clarity the drink will give, as I put my hangover aside.

"Alright." He slowed. The sun was just barely up; it must have been about 6 in the morning when we reached the mall's entrance. I opened the door.

"I never got your name, oh wise one," I said as I stepped onto the sidewalk.

"Why do you care? You'll forget me as soon as you light another smoke." He handed me another one. "The name is... Ivan. Ivan the terrible."

"Ha. Good day, sir. Watch out for that looming mid-life crisis," I said as I closed the door.

CHAPTER 2

I walked to a bench with just a little light hitting it. I sat, smoked, and then turned to observe the town awakening. I like people in the mornings, especially in the downtown core. Not so much the mornings themselves, but the feel of people moving about with a purpose. Make a little money and then die. Still, I admired their walks that said, 'I have somewhere to go. I'll walk fast so that all can understand my importance.'

My mind turned over again to the thought of more

coffee. Zenari's must be open at this hour. I could get some more coffee and maybe a bite; feeling hungry this time of day was strange for me. I got up, throwing the smoke down, and walked into the intersection as the light turned green. I peered over at the important people having to wait. Maybe Rebecca was working. Maybe I could get a free coffee and see what she had to say about working and living. Experienced at both, she worked mornings and went to school in the afternoons. School: another empty activity. You get a degree, make some more money and then die. Post-secondary served no purpose. Everything they teach you is in books, so why not just buy the books and save the money? Forced learning is something you pay for to call yourself a specialist. Special at what? Special at learning? Special at living? I'm special at living. I hold all the tools I need to conquer this world: a smoke in one hand, a skull ring on the other and a bottle of bourbon never out of reach.

The cafe was open and I let out a sigh. I decided I did need more coffee, but no food. Rebecca was running about behind the counter. The owner was there having some coffee himself. He glanced up at me like I was homeless and gave out a snort of annoyance—but then again at the end of the day all the extra muffins do go to the homeless.

"Hey, Rebecca," I called as I walked in. They must have just opened.

"What the hell do you want?" She must have still been pissed about the party where I left her to hold my drink, never to return, in my typical fashion. Her medium-length hair had a purple streak running through it.

"You left me at Olson's party with an unpaid." She leant forward, "A hundred dollars' worth. I should have sent the dealer after you, you snake."

I smiled. "Rebecca. Apologies. I had to leave when the skinheads showed up. You know what your brother thought of our relationship, being so clean-shaved himself."

"You're still a bastard." The owner of the store looked up with alarm.

"Listen I could have taken him out. It's just that they travel in packs, those fascists." I stood back.

"I don't want to cause a scene, but you owe me fifty dollars. You got it, or not?"

"Come outside with me. I'm having one hell of a start today. Come outside and have a smoke. Just not in here, 'cause your manager seems to object to my appearance."

"As he should. You look like you woke up in a ditch. It's an improvement."

"Ah, Rebecca, you have no idea the morning I've had," I said as I put my hand on her side and directed her out of the cafe, through the mall, and out onto the sidewalk. "And hey, your powers of observation haven't failed you. I did wake up in a ditch. You weren't at the Afeller show, were you? Something weird happened last night, and I was hoping you could shed some light on it."

It wasn't until I felt the water on my face that I realized she had a glass in her hand.

"You asshole. You left me to pay that bastard. He almost broke my arm."

I wiped the water from my face and lit a smoke. "C'mon, I had to get out of there. You know the skinheads are out to get me."

"You don't seem to have many friends these days. Not surprising, the way you treat people. Now put down your smoke for a second."

I lowered the cigarette, and she slapped my face.

"Jesus, Rebecca, that really sucked."

"You have till the end of the day to pay me back, or I'll give my brothers your mother-fucking coordinates and they'll kick the shit out of you."

I picked my sunglasses up and looked at her. She stood fuming. I gave an honest shrug. The anger in her face seemed to fade as we stared at each other.

"I meant you no harm. I would do everything in my power to keep you safe. You are wild—but tame to me. Come on, Lois Lane. You know how you used to smile when you saw me; your face would light up like fireworks. Did all that go away just because of some money? Is that all the merit I hold in your eyes?"

The sun peered around a building, and we stood in a perfect ray, it felt like the change in temperature was just for us.

"Rebecca," I said again. Her face softened and a small smile crept across it, then she jumped into my arms.

"Oh, my Superman."

"Rebecca, soon we'll get out of this town together." I smiled. Half of it was true.

"I have to get back. I like you."

"And I like you, Rebecca," I said as I brushed her cheek with the back of my hand.

"You *are* going to the show tonight?" she asked.

"I wouldn't miss it."

She walked back inside. I threw my butt to the ground.

CHAPTER 3

I went to a little tobacco shop and bought two packs of Peter Jackson Specials—the strength of ten cigarettes in one. Then I headed to a small bench overlooking my city's river valley. It has one of the largest inner city parks in North America, I'm told by people that are grasping at straws to justify living in a metropolis so far north—further north than Moscow. I remember watching movies about Russia in the Cold War; films in black and white, the people freezing, waves of snow built around them as they waited in line to get bread. That kind of bleak cold made Russia seem like the worst

13

place on earth to live, and here we live further north than the cities in those movies. But we have a big park, and it was summer, so people seemed to forget how harsh our winter is. Me? I'm thick-skinned. A leather jacket in minus forty is all I need. I even ride my motorcycle through the winter. Take that, you former Soviets.

I sat on the bench staring at the sun for as long as I could before my eyes stung with pain. I took out the bottle and took a few short swigs. It wasn't even eight, and yet already I was getting myself back into a clear state of thinking. An old homeless man was sitting a few benches down from me. I could tell he was going to ask me for a smoke. The man got up awkwardly and started shuffling down the walkway pretending not to notice me. I played a counting game in my head as he approached. 'Three.' He stood not five feet from me; his grey hair contrasted well with his long black jacket, his strong large hands half in his pockets. 'Two.' Right beside me, asking if he could sit and I said fine. 'One.'

"Hey there, mind if I could get one of those off you?"

"Sure thing, pop," I said.

"How are you doing? You're not one of those skinheads, are you?"

"No. Everyone is equal… even though they aren't, really."

"That's how I feel. The mayor's daughter and I are on the same page, yes, but if I go missing, people might look for a day if they even notice. She goes missing and the city gets turned upside down. Equal rights, they say. Ha. I noticed you're drinking. Have a little to spare? Where did you get a bottle so early?" I pulled out the bottle and passed it to him.

"You know those well-to-do middle-class men? Well, they are quite the drinkers. I got it off one of them," I said.

"Well, man, they say it changes, but it never does. Martin Luther King and the rest brought about change. But equality for the poor... Doesn't change. It just divides the rich and the poor even more. Me and you are on different pages—different levels of importance. It's not just money that separates me from the mayor's daughter; it's my mind, you know. That's the real divider. Our prisons are filled with nutjobs. That's something that needs to be addressed." He took a long swig; a longer one then I would have liked.

"It's money, man. It's all about money. Your quality of life isn't that bad, I'm sure. At least in the summer, eh? Why don't you move west?"

"And deal with the nicer weather? The thought has crossed my mind. I could panhandle enough to get a bus ticket. But this is my home. This is where I'll die. You know, you get old and you just find the beauty in this city. You don't understand. I'm sure you just want to get out of here. But yet, you stay."

"Yeah, I stay. There's a quote I like, goes something like... umm... Shit. I can never remember these things."

"Ha ha. Your mind's going, eh? What's your name, son?"

"My name?" I paused, knowing the answer had little meaning, especially with this guy. "My name is Clark Kent."

"Ah, I see. And you're immune from corruption and hostility? You have super powers, don't you?" he laughed. "Can you spare some change? This bottle is making me remember fond times when I was a young superhero like yourself."

I moved my hands through my coat; I hadn't explored the pockets that well this morning. Then I felt something hard in a hidden pocket I had sewn into my jacket for sneaking drugs and such into shows. What the hell? I had a hard time pulling it out of the pocket. As I looked back at the old man, I pulled out a money clip as thick as a small paperback. The kind that I would find too long to read.

"Holy shit," the man said. "Who *are* you?"

There must have been five thousand dollars. I just stared at the hundreds and fifties. What happened last night? This wasn't mine. I'd never seen so much money in my life.

"Like I told you... I'm Clark Kent," I said, still staring at the money in disbelief.

"You're not a drug dealer, are you?"

"No. Drugs aren't my thing."

I lit another smoke and looked back at the river. I must have gotten into a quite a shit show—or I was definitely headed into one. I must have stolen it at the show; whoever this money belonged to would be looking for it. Did they know I had it?

"You could go far with money like that. You know what I'd do?"

"Prostitutes and liquor."

"Ha. No, Clark, I would give it to my daughter for college."

I couldn't help but laugh. "You were married?"

"No, but I had a daughter. She must be..." He was counting the years on his hands. "She must be an adult now. Her mother was—*is* a druggie. My daughter, though, wouldn't touch the stuff. She looked after her mom after I left. A smart girl could go on to do great things, and I know she will, but she needs schooling."

"A daughter, eh?"

"Yeah, Ellie."

"Why did you leave her to look after your old lady?"

"I had to Clark, I'm..." He looked away, "I see things. I see the world, you know."

"You're fucked in the head, aren't you?"

"Mental illness destroys you. In and out of the hospital—in and out of institutions. Kills a family and it just screws up everything."

"Listen, man. I don't know how this money got into my jacket. Didn't know I had it. Don't really care that I do. Take this money to that bank down the street; put it in your daughter's account. Write a letter, a well-written letter, for this Ellie. Tell her you're sorry."

"No, Clark, I couldn't possibly take that money. I just couldn't."

"Listen, man. I'm not asking. You've led a messy life

17

I'm sure you hurt a ton of people. I know the type. Do this for me and get your grubby hands off my bourbon." I snatched the bottle away, threw the money in his lap, tossed my smoke to the ground, and started to walk away.

"Hey Clark. Clark Kent."

"Shut up. You sound crazy," I said, leaving him behind. Ellie. Tough life. Hope that helps. I still had to figure out what went down last night. I had to see what the guys were up to. This was a mess; more of a mess than I was used to. Anybody carrying that cash wasn't up to any good. And look at me: I just did a social service. I'm such a nice guy.

CHAPTER 4

I walked across downtown to a small parkade with a stall that I rented. No fixed address, but if someone wanted to track me down they could find the bike. I wasn't lying about the bike that morning and I pictured the Harley in all her glory as I worked my way up the stairs. My father had it coming. He would never report it stolen; he knew that nothing good would come of that. I swung my leg over and released the kickstand—didn't bother with a helmet. I sped out across the parkade and shot out the bottom like from a loaded assault rifle. The wind was on my face as I worked my way up through the gears, jesting at cars as I passed them.

The night before didn't make sense. This had something to do with the 'heads, I was sure. If I took the money from them, they would be out for blood. But it couldn't have been; I'm not that stupid. The guys at the loft might have some answers. The thing about last night that worried me was I was really out of my element; my mind was out on my sleeve, and I was unusually vulnerable. Didn't know the crowd.

As I drove, small flashes of the evening came back: It was a good show. I remembered looking towards the door after the band finished. I was with some girl. Who was she? Flashes of red hair, blue eyes, and lots of freckles. We did some pills. I remembered seeing the drugs in my hand, but I didn't remember taking them. What happened? A group of 'heads came in the back door. I tried to focus my semi-intoxicated brain as I rode the bike, but I couldn't make too much from the brief flashes. All I could remember was the girl, the band finishing their set, the drugs in my hand, and the 'heads walking in. That was all.

I crossed the High Level Bridge. On Canada Day, they send a waterfall over the side. It was the kind of massive waste of water that only a red-necked Albertan could love. But that wasn't the only reason I loved the bridge: it was also the sharp *S* at the top of the hill. Throttle wide open as you ride up the perfect end to a bridge.

I didn't have far to go to reach the loft off campus. I don't know how Matt and Mike got the place; couldn't see how they could afford it. But they did, somehow, and it was as good a place as any to rest my head, maybe get some more drinks in me, and find some answers: the girl, the 'heads, and the strange-looking pills.

I parked the bike, lit another smoke, and walked up to their door. It was only then that I realized how early it was: just past eight or so. They must be sleeping or, if I was lucky, still up from the night before. If I was even luckier, they would have been at the same event as me—lost in the crowd. I pushed their buzzer for what seemed like an eternity. When hung over, loud noises and time are different. You would live forever if annoying sounds were going off in your ear at all hours of the day. I should write a book about that; screw eating healthy, not drinking, and not smoking. The key to longevity: just listen to long annoying sounds at all hours.

Finally, I was let in. Another smile crossed my face; lucky three times before eight a.m. Hopefully, that wouldn't be the end of my luck.

CHAPTER 5

I smoked in the elevator, knowing it's not allowed. I thought about the perpetual mess things were in—not me or last night but just the order in this world. I thought of the man who gave me a lift that morning: how he said he was like me, how he said one day I'd be like him. The thought kind of stuck, though I told myself it shouldn't concern me since all I saw in my future was a string of good times and women tied together with punk rock. In my view, punk was going to have as big an impact in the underground as the flower movement of the '60s. Punk rock was the future—the optimal way to live your life. The speed of life just needs some background music, and that music is punk. Getting yourself in trouble and having a good story to tell were often one and the same; last night might just be a story of a man who finds a lot of cash and gives it to a homeless man who promises to give it to his estranged daughter so she can lead the kind of life I found so dull and uninspired. The background music to a life like that would surely be classical, maybe jazz if there was a little zest, but nothing like punk.

The door to the lift opened and I stared into an empty loft. It always looked half destroyed: chairs turned over, empty pizza boxes and Chinese take-out all over the place. No one came to greet me. They must have been sleeping. Maybe the bender of the weekend had not yet started—but it was Friday, so I had hope.

I walked through the loft over to a sectioned-off bedroom: Mike's room.

"Hey Mike, get up. Let's have some coffee, a drink, and a smoke," I said as I looked at the dark cot. A large figure with a blanket barely covering their naked body didn't move, but I knew it was him. I walked over and shook his torso, but still nothing. So, for the moment, I gave up. As I walked into the kitchen, I heard talking in the other room. It sounded like Matt and some girl. I walked over to their part of the sectioned-off living space. It must have been them who buzzed me in.

"Hey, Matt," I said. He was just pulling up his pants and the girl, probably some blond from the University, was in her underwear and was content with sleeping. Matt had a shaved head with stripes running down the side and two slightly different-coloured eyes. He always said it helped him break the ice when it came to meeting random girls.

"Hey, man," he was holding his head. "You just had to ring that goddamn buzzer. Fuck, do you know what time it is? God."

"Nice to see you too. I had kind of an interesting start to the day. I think I was thrown out of a car last night and I woke up in a ditch." I would feel things out before I told him everything I knew. "Who's the girl?" I asked.

"Um, can't for the life of me remember her name." He stood up and gave me a firm punch to the shoulder then lit a smoke. "What can I do for you, man?"

"I'm looking for a few answers about last night. Something crazy went down. Were you at the Afeller show?"

"Me? No… I bet Mike was. Let's wake him." He walked into the kitchen and filled a large pot with ice-cold water while he hummed a tune.

We stood above the sleeping Mike holding the pot of water with cigarettes hanging out of our mouths. "Rise and shine, Mike," Matt said as he dumped the water on the figure who cried out and sprang up soaking wet holding a switchblade. He lunged at Matt and pinned him against the wall with the knife at his neck. I stepped back a bit but wasn't that worried. Still panting as water dripped down his head and onto the floor, he lowered the knife.

"You bastard. You mother fucker."

Matt just laughed. *Psycho Mike* as he is known in the community.

"And fuck you, too," Mike said looking at me. I was laughing and gave him a smoke. "Well, I'm up now! Don't you even think about telling what time it is. Fuck!"

"Listen, man, I had a hell of a morning and was wondering about the show last night—the Afeller show. Do you remember any of it or seeing me there?" He stabbed the knife into a small drawer still standing naked. "Parts of it I remember, yeah… I think saw you. I was out of my element at that show with all the 'heads."

"I need to know what you remember. I'll run down to the store and grab us some coffees," I said, walking to the lift. Matt and Mike sat down on the couch and started rolling a joint. "And hey... save some of that for me."

"You best hurry, then."

CHAPTER 6

"Three black coffees," I said putting coins on the counter.

"Anything else for you, hun?"

Hun? Who was she calling *hun*? "Ah, no. A tray, though."

I took the coffees and headed back to the loft. *Hun*? Did I look like I was selling cookies? I poured out some of my coffee and added the last of the bourbon. I walked past an attractive blond who smiled at me. Why did she smile? And why was I being called *hun*? I needed to get a face tattoo or a piercing—or both.

Something to redirect the smiles and terms of endearment. Friendliness was unsettling; it bothered me. Made me think that people had stopped fearing my crew.

I got to the top of the lift and walked back in. The guys passed me their joint, then I passed out the coffees.

"The lady… called me *hun* at the coffee shop. Has she ever called you guys hun?"

They smiled weak pot smiles.

"*Hun*, she called you? Strange, but maybe that's the kind of nickname that will catch on in the community," Matt said as he smirked.

"I don't think anyone has ever called me hun. Grandmother used to call me *The Abomination*. that always seemed to fit as I was usually caught going through her medicine cabinet; old bird was the first investor in my high-school prescription pill venture. *Abomination* fits. *Hun* doesn't fit."

"You need a face tattoo," Mike said, taking a deep drag.

"Yeah, that's what I was thinking. Misfit skull right on the forehead."

"That would be sweet," Matt said.

"Any-fucking-ways. Let's talk about how I ended up in a ditch last night. Mike: Any ideas?"

"That's a good question. There was some bad shit going around at that show. The 'heads were feeding the crowd with pills and lines. There was one guy in particular that was being generous, like he won the lotto or something. Can't remember his name, but he had a crew of bikers with him. You were talking with them… The older biker didn't say much. I'd never seen him before, but I was so strung out that by the end of the show I was drifting in and out. Hmmm. Now that I think of it, I saw you with some redhead; an artist at the U who seemed to know the new Afeller drummer. Watched you leave with Mr. Generous, the old biker, and the band. I stumbled back here and smoked weed until I fell asleep."

"Sounds just like a typical show for me. So I left with some 'heads and the band—and you didn't know any of those randoms?"

"No, man, they seemed like a heavy crowd even for you. Maybe you OD'd and they left you for dead."

"My head was hurting something fierce this morning." I didn't think to tell them about the cash, but the information Mike gave me was a touch unsettling.

"I'd find that girl. I talked to her a bit. She did say she was in school doing her Masters in Fine Arts. She might be there today. Summer school or some shit… I'd pry man."

"Yeah, you might leave with a number. 'Course you got no home phone, you drifter," Matt said.

"Hey now, I was thinking of getting a phone set up in my parking stall; set up a tent, have a nice life."

"Man, with that bike you could go anywhere. It's fucking summer. What are you still doing here? Go to Cali or something. Get out of dodge."

"Yeah, you're right. I just love the music scene

here. I'll leave when the time is right."

"If you woke up in a ditch, maybe that time is now. The 'heads are making the city whiter, running fear every day. Doesn't bode well with me, man."

"Maybe, but from what you've told me there's a hot redhead. I'll have to visit the University, god-awful place it is to be strung out in. Hopefully, she won't be like Rebecca who threw water in my face this morning."

"She's still bitter about that party? That girl's got issues," Matt put in. "Let's roll another joint and pour a few more morning beers."

We sat and talked some more, but all I wanted to do was get out of that loft and see this girl, so I didn't hang out too much longer. I was betting she would still be in her studio, using it through the summer as some artist. When I left the loft, it was still early. I was drunk, stoned, and in a good mood for some flirting.

CHAPTER 7

I walked from the loft towards the school, a bit of a skip in my step, hoping to find some decent answers. I was feeling pretty good until I saw some guy handing out flyers. "I have no time for these people," I thought—and considered saying it out loud as he approached.

"God is all around us, son. Even those who drift from the path find welcome in the arms of Christianity if they accept Jesus Christ as their Savior," he said, handing me a flyer.

"Fuck off, eh?"

Religious types always freaked me out, especially the extreme ones. On another day I would have laid into him, but I had a better purpose today. When I was stoned, I could talk—I had opinions—but when I was sober, my tongue didn't work. I pulled another smoke from the half-empty pack and started to walk towards the campus. I'd dated enough college girls to know that right next to the law section was the 'Arts' building. Finishing my smoke, I entered and started snooping around. Maybe this girl would have an art studio. I checked to see if she was in printmaking, but had no luck and kept looking. I saw the cover of a newspaper half-crumpled on the ground: a story about a gang-related homicide, and for a moment my thoughts wandered back to what Mike had talked about and the money I woke up with in my coat.

CHAPTER 8

"You partied pretty hard last night." The redhead was drawing as I entered the studio. She had square-framed glasses and didn't look at me as she talked. The room was hardly private as it was shared with other artists, all in semi-enclosed spaces.

"Yeah, I guess I did. I heard you were with me—and now that I see your face, I recognize you a bit. Can you shed a little light on what happened?"

"You've got some nerve. You sure didn't give me much to remember you by." She put the pencil down from her sketchbook and finally looked up at me.

"Come on, shed a little light. Was I that bad?"

She laughed. "Well, asshole, you left me in the bathroom waiting for you as you ran off to score some drugs. You never returned. The things I would have done to you would make all those Albertan girls look like a joke, and now you'll never know what you missed out on."

"Wow. You're the second girl to call me an asshole before noon, so you don't have the glory of winning the day quite yet," I said as I pulled up a chair beside her. "Although you're the more attractive girl to call me an asshole, so I must admit: coming from you, it hurts a bit more—but just a bit, so don't go running to your friends bragging. God, you're an art type. Are you trying to change the world through your art or are you just trying to become famous? Not rich, because artists don't become rich—they become famous—which also means that I made you feel a little famous last night." With that, she slapped me.

"You can go to hell. Who the hell do you think you are? Some big shot punk rocker with nothing to his name; you may think you're 'scene famous' in Edmonton for some unknown reason, but I had never heard of you before."

"I'm one of a kind, babe."

"You came here looking for answers. But even if I had anything to tell you, after that speech—after you just proclaimed to have not only my life but my art completely figured out—I have only one answer for you: crawl back down the drunken, drug-induced rabbit hole you came from. Better yet, do the world a favour and overdose."

I lit up a smoke and sat back in my chair.

"You can't smoke in here. Put that out!"

I dropped the smoke in what looked like

someone's water.

"Listen, I'm going to come to this studio till you tell me about last night. I'm going to come here smoke and drink and…"

"And what?"

And I started singing. Horribly. The kind of notes that don't exist for a reason. Everyone stopped working.

"Stop, stop… alright! Shit, man."

But I kept on singing. When I finally stopped, I looked over at her and laughed. "And I'll light this place up like an opera house every day until you tell me about those guys we were with. Did I leave with them? I woke up in a ditch this morning—so level with me."

She shook her head and whispered, "Alright, but promise me never to come back here." She paused and then lowered her voice again. "Those guys kept talking about a hit and about getting a lot of money for doing someone a big favour. You kept telling them where they could get some good stuff to take their night to another level and you kept going on about what a connoisseur you were. Um… Two of them wore biker jackets; the younger one was buying everyone lines and flashing his money around."

"Do you know their names? Anything about where they were from? Anything at all?"

"They said that they were going to party all weekend and meet at The Bronx with some 'heads who they owe money to. You left with them in a black, beaten-down Cadillac heading out of the city."

"The Bronx tonight, eh? It's another Afeller show,"

I said as the pieces started to fall into place. We must have gone to the farm for an after-party. "And the band left with us?"

"Yeah, the band followed you. I only know this because I left the bathroom to see the convoy of cars leave with you in the lead. Where did you go?"

"Hmmm. I can't really recall. There's some stuff I need to check out. Why don't you come to The Bronx tonight? I can repay you a little."

"You think you deserve another chance with me?"

I took off my sunglasses and stared at her. "I must have said something to get you to go to that bathroom; what did I say?"

"That's for me to know and for you to remember. If you think anything like that will happen tonight, you'll be disappointed. As you must think, given the condition of your life, sadness breeds your purpose."

I got up and headed for the door, "Sadness breeds creativity," I said, my voice empty as I turned and left.

I would have to go to the farm. It seemed the bikers from last night had money to pay the 'heads and now they are deprived of that money—now some girl named Ellie's money.

CHAPTER 9

Before I walked to my bike, I quickly popped into the loft to let the guys know that I'd stop by to gather them up before going to The Bronx. The farm was my uncle's, and I only showed my face there with people when I was out to impress. I don't know why but as I passed a pay phone I had a strange rush—an unusual urgency— and at that moment I figured I'd give my mother a call. It's something I rarely did. I don't know why the urge to call rose up inside of me; I hadn't spoken to mom in almost four months. I slowly dropped the coins into the phone, hearing them hit the bottom of the bin. I punched in the numbers and sparked a smoke to tide me through the call.

"Hello," said a woman's voice through some coughing.

"Eh, mom. it's me."

"I see... I've been trying to get in touch with you."

"Have you, now... And to what do I owe that privilege?"

"Your father, Joe... he died. Last week. The service is today. I'd like you to attend and maybe speak."

"Where?" I asked flatly as the news hit me, letting my voice show nothing.

"A small place by your uncle's farm. It would mean a lot if you came. I know you and Joe had differences, but it would mean a lot to me." She maintained a small cough the whole time she was talking. I could hear the seal of a what I knew was a bottle of bourbon cracking and a drink being poured. "And I wouldn't worry about the bike; consider it yours. He would have wanted you to have it anyways. Where are you staying? What are you doing for money?"

"It's at that church, right?" I asked, ignoring her questions.

"Yes, at two o'clock."

"I'll be there."

"Hey, wait." I heard her say as I put the phone down and just stared at it for a while. I couldn't believe the man had died. Didn't matter how. I looked at the ground as I lit another smoke. The man was dead. Maybe from an overdose—probably from an overdose. My mother sounded like she was on her way out as well. I just stood there. Someone banged on the glass waiting to use the phone; I ignored him.

"Hey, punk. Are you finished? I have to make an important call!" I ignored the voice behind me and just stared at the phone. "Come on. What are you doing in there? Get out of the booth!" He started to open the door. I turned and faced him.

"Come on, you punk, get out of there." He grabbed my jacket. With all my force, I pushed him backwards. He was much larger, but I was much stronger. As I pushed him back, the rage in my body overpowered him and I pushed him to the ground. My fist raised to hit him with everything in me, I held back and then starting to run. My thoughts were jumbled. Joe was dead. I'd wanted it that way for many years. Now, faced with it, I saw my father everywhere I looked. The world, him, and his fucking generation. I saw his face in everyone as I ran until my lungs burned and my legs ached. I ran right into a liquor store, panting.

"Son," the clerk said, the words hitting me as if I was the son of everybody now.

I didn't acknowledge him as I picked up a bottle of whisky. "Brown bag."

CHAPTER 10

I walked the streets, taking hefty swigs. Joe, the man at the centre of my hate, was dead. The man who controlled the world, who brought my sense of being to an apocalypse, was dead. My mind blurred with my thoughts of the man. I couldn't seem to come up with any good emotions. Just hatred—and betrayal over the knowledge that now I was expected to send him off to the next world. In his case, it was more likely that he would be reincarnated as another hate-filled, drug-abusing man who would surely live the same way and drive away the same son. Lead us not into temptation, but deliver us from evil. The bottle was doing an unfortunate job of amplifying the emotions that I was so reluctant to feel—these thoughts that haunted me.

I pushed the bottle up to my lips and felt the whisky burn its way down, a smoke still held in my mouth. I didn't wince; just like my father, I thought. Was I like him? Maybe I was heading down the same path as he did. The notion filled me with anger because there was no way I was like him. The little I knew about the man was the anger he instilled in me. I was self-destructive, yes, but he was a human destroyer and everything that embodied. I had always envisioned dying in my prime so that he would have to bury me. The man would have to gather his courage in the same church I was heading to later and confess that he made me this way. That he was the knife; he was the catalyst. People didn't seem to care as I lowered myself against a building. Students and early-morning shoppers walked by without a second glance—or they didn't look at all. Just another life ready to die. I saw an officer approaching and quickly hid the bottle in a small bush, but he just walked past. Why would he care? He knew people like me were not meant to waste time on. Guys like me were above the law, but only because we lined the bottom. I sat and smoked and a few people threw some change at my feet, which I collected. If I saw the homeless man again, I would give it to him for his daughter. For the life of me, I couldn't remember her name anymore. Would I become like Joe? No, I wasn't anything like my father. I tried to pull myself together quickly and stood, forcing on my jacket, then gathered my thoughts and stumbled a little.

"Hey. You okay, son?" An old man asked. I just blankly looked at him. There was that word again. In what way was I his son? My father was the only person who could call me that. Even if he was here and he wouldn't.

"Yeah, pop, I'm fine."

"Hey, let me buy you some food. It would be no trouble." I looked up at him and saw a clean-shaven man with dull grey eyes under unkempt eyebrows. He had the look of a kind man; the kind that shows pity on the godless.

"Alright, old man, but... don't call me son."

"Okay, sure thing."

I smiled. Why were such people approaching me? Why were they smiling at me? There must have been something in the air—something about this day. I walked with the man who was already mentioning something about looking at a flower and asking me how a flower could be made without a god. I wasn't actually listening, nor walking in much of a straight line.

We headed a little way down Whyte Avenue until he held open a door and showed me to a table. I was full of alcohol, so food would likely do me some good if I could keep it down.

"What can I get for you? Coffee?" The server asked. I raised my arm as if to gesture that I wanted a drink, but the man stopped me.

"Two coffees please. Black."

I laughed and looked back at him.

"Son... I mean, sorry. It's early, and you look three sheets to the wind. I'm surprised I didn't have to bring you in here in a wheelbarrow, so you're having a coffee."

I looked back at him with a drunken smile on my face. Why did these men come into my life? Why was every man my father? Every man but the one I was burying.

"You know what, man, I'm not even going to fight you on that one because I have a feeling that this will be my last day on earth."

"Why would you say something like that?"

"Things that have happened today that are leading me to think my time is almost over," I answered as our coffees arrived.

"Is that so? Well then, since you're getting a free meal out of me, allow me this chance to try and help you."

"I don't need saving," I said as my head swayed. "Life is just an assortment of events: complex, great and pointless. The way this day started and the way it's continuing have made for an eventful day; the kind that, for me, could only have two ends."

"In what ways could it end?" He asked.

"I don't know... It'll end with me riding off into the

sunset with a dame or two... or with some old man saying a few words and people taking turns throwing dirt."

"I'm sorry to hear that. The day I discovered the Lord my saviour was like that. Would you like to hear about that day? It might shed a little light on what you're going through now. Maybe there's a third route to this day. Maybe this is the day you meet your saviour."

I thought back on the money, the girls, the 'heads, the bikers, and the point it was going to come to. I looked around in a brief moment of calm and thought that people were probably out looking for me. Hunting me. Maybe their intent was to finish what they started when they left me for dead. I looked across at this man I had just met. I didn't need the free meal he was providing to meet some saviour. No, what I needed was to cut a deal with the other saviour; the one deep beneath the earth that is who I should have been calling out to this whole time.

"Can I get you something to eat?" A short Chinese waitress asked us. "Or just some more coffee for you two?"

The man answered, "Yes, we'll have some more coffee, some fried squid, sticky rice, shrimp toast, pork dumplings and black bean greens," he said as he scanned the menu. "Anything you want to add?"

"Yeah, some General Tso's chicken and some... never mind, that's all good." The waitress took our order and left us to the literal god-awful conversation we were having. The things I would do for a meal.

"So would you like to hear about that day?"

"The day you met your saviour?"

"Yes."

"Sure, why not kill a little time. Time is for the killing."

He placed both hands on the table and closed his eyes for a moment. Another fanatic, I thought.

"Well, I was into drugs, and already had one overdose to my name. I was young and thought I was bulletproof—and for a time, I was. Good at dodging bullets, that is. So, after what seemed like a three-day bender, I had collapsed in a gutter. No one came to help; I just looked up at the stars. The world was overlooking my existence. No one stopped. I told myself I would just lay there until the goodness of men was proven. I would just lie there hoping that the human race would help me. I spent the night watching people walk by. I felt as if I was invisible and, finally, I had accepted my lot. But then, at my lowest moment, a little girl eating some candy approached me. She must have been on her way to school. I still remember her face as she said 'Mister, get up. God doesn't frown on people every day. Only sometimes when they've been bad. But God looks after all people, and he'll look after you.' And with that, this fearless girl reached out her hand. It was as if angels filled her body and gave her the strength of ten men to pull me free from that gutter. There was no way she could have lifted me up, but she did. Ever since that day I have been clean, honest, and kind to all that appear in the situation I was in."

He looked back at me and our food had just started to arrive. I was holding my chopsticks; my interest was waning from the table.

"I see," I said. "So you seek out those who were like you. You're saying I need to be more like you are now. You're saying that there is a God and you met him in that girl."

"Yes,"

"Well, man, I like your story and I can see why you choose to tell it, but the thing with me is I wouldn't lie in that gutter like you did. I would have gotten up and gone back to the party," I said as I started eating. My composure was beginning to clear up.

"Come on now, you must see that the life you're living will send you to the devil and an early death. You must be aware in moments of clarity that soon you will die. You just told me how close to the end you feel on this very day."

"Yes, but you know who I'll meet tonight? I'll meet people like me. People who care about me. People are my saviours: they make me better, stronger, and smarter. You say that the girl pulled you up. Well, I've met God hundreds of times: he's in the face of my friends and in people I meet. God is in everyone. God is in you just as much as he is in me, heaven is on earth, and the devil is on my shoulder just the same. It only depends on whether or not I feed him. God is also on my shoulder. I'm not a complete atheist. Don't rightly think anyone is; that's just a way to shock people. To shut them up. Guys like you, no offence. I mean you just bought me some of my favourite food. But when God tells me what to do I choose to listen to the devil, because this is our heaven here on earth. This is our one shot at life. We're just the souls from some parallel universe. And when we die, we're just recycled to another universe, which may be better or worse. Hell, maybe this is the worst universe for us, and it only gets better. All I know is you only have one life. This is mine, and that's yours so let's enjoy the rest of our food, then I'll go one way, you'll go another, and we will never meet again."

His eyebrows dropped, and he didn't say anything else. We did as I said and finished eating. He paid the bill and we walked out of the restaurant going in different directions. I felt better; still kind of drunk, which would make riding a bit more exciting. I would enjoy the short ride out of town, then bury the man I never called my father.

CHAPTER 11

I disregarded the man's story and tried to focus more on the day. I wondered who would come to the funeral; I was sure Joe had driven away the few friends he'd had. I started riding out into the country and I raced down Whyte Avenue towards Sherwood Park. My thoughts were muddled about my father. I tried to think of something good, but even from a young age he treated me so shitty. Could I just rip him down at his funeral? That would stroke my ego just a little bit too much, and that wasn't the way of punk rock. The earliest memory I had was of two guys who tried to break into our house. I came down the stairs to see my father in his underwear, pushing them out the door with a loaded, unregistered .22. 'You've got the wrong house,' he said, causing the would-be thieves to trip and fall backwards over themselves. Then there was a memory of the one time we went fishing and he wouldn't help me bring in a fish. I was about nine and struggled for an hour while he just kept saying, "Man up, son," as he sipped his beer in our rented boat. "You'll never get anywhere in life if this little fish can out-think you." Eventually, I dropped the rod in the water; the fish had won. He then pushed me in laughing and shouting, "Swim back!" then paddled the boat away. That was the way the man was. I left home at seventeen, taking his bike while he was passed out on the couch. My mother was crying in the kitchen because he had just put a beat on me for not coming home the night before, and that was it. I was gone. Was that all I could remember of the man? We would now never have that classic man-to-man talk, with beers and apologies—his father made him, etcetera.

I left the county of Sherwood Park and then took a few service roads, racing along train tracks and cutting onto other dirt roads without a real plan. But I knew I would end up at the church. Who would be there? What would I say? I hoped it wasn't going to be a big Catholic service. Joe would always say this old cliché about church: "Carry me in at birth, drag me in at marriage, and wheel me in at death." That was about the extent it.

I stopped my bike a half kilometre away, checked my pockets and again I thought of the time with the fish. What kind of man would do that to his son? What kind of man was he? I would never find out now. The most flattering thing I could think of was the man's passion for the Oilers and their playoff streak a few years back in the 80's with their golden boy, Gretzky. That was a good memory. I found the small joint I was looking for; I had swiped it from Mike and Matt's place. I'd now reached that point when you drink during the day where you either need to keep going or stop and get a little high.

I sat watching the smoke float away. Since they say

you turn into your father, I was never having children. I felt I owed it to the world to stop this bloodline. Taking long drags, I smoked the joint down to a roach. I could feel the pump up it gave me. My headache went away and my mind cleared of all thoughts. This was the perfect place to be for public speaking. I figured there wouldn't be too many people there anyways. My worries about the 'heads and the biker gang—and surely the mini-manhunt that was going on as they looked for their hit money—all faded away. I thought a bit about the two girls I had invited to The Bronx. Hopefully, this was going to be the start of a good bender. If everything went to plan, I'd be able to leave The Bronx without a scratch and get rid of a few 'heads in the process. That would, I smiled, make my old man pretty happy.

CHAPTER 12

I got back on the bike and headed up to the church. I loved to ride the bike stoned. I'd almost forgotten, but after whatever service was to come, I would have to make a stop at my uncle's farm and ask him about his take on the previous night. Then I thought about maybe going to see the guitarist from the Afellers, my oldest friend. Maybe he could also be of some help.

My mother was outside waiting for me, dressed in black with a veil she must have spent all of her bottle money on. As much as I disliked my father, I could never figure out why she loved the guy so much. She would never stand up for me. It was as if I was the reason their lives slowed; I was the reason they gave up a good life. I parked the bike as she approached, smoking a slim 100. I lit a cigarette as well.

"Hey, you made it."

"Yeah."

"Good to see you. Are you doing okay? Eating?"

"Yeah, Mom, I'm fine. I eat."

"So why did you spend money on getting yourself a greasy Mohawk if you never put in the effort to stand it up?"

"Women can spend time in front of the mirror, but it's pretty lame if I do."

"I see you haven't changed. What are you doing for money?"

"I traffic illegal immigrants," I said, already disliking the conversation. "What are you doing for money? You still partying hard?"

"Oh, shut up."

"Well, Mom, I can see that you haven't grown up either. So what's the deal? You want me to speak?"

"Well, I did. I figured you have a little insight on the man. I can't because I hate talking in front of groups. So the buck falls on you."

"What are you afraid of? There's no one even in there. I've seen, like, five people go inside."

"Just be a man this one time... You wouldn't happen to have any cash, would you?"

"Ah, I did have a few thousand dollars this morning, but a homeless man beat you to the punch."

"What!?"

"I'm just kidding."

There was just over a large handful of people inside the church. Even though it was small, it still looked empty. I took a seat near the back beside an apparently-lost blonde close to my age. My mother walked past me and sat at the front.

"Hey, how's it going?" I asked the girl. She looked a little familiar, like I had met her at a party or we had gone to school together. "What on earth are you doing here?" I asked again when she didn't respond to my first question.

"My dad was Joe's old friend. I'm here for him because he always spoke highly of the guy."

I looked at her again, "Are you sure you're in the right place."

"Yes, I am. What are you here for, the free coffee?"

"Something like that... I had one hell of a night. Figured I need a little sanctuary."

She smiled. "What's your name?"

"Me? Clark Kent. Yours?"

"Silk Spectre."

"I like a girl with good taste in comic books."

She shushed me as a priest stood at the front and started to speak. I rolled my eyes.

CHAPTER 13

I would learn later that it was my estranged grandmother who paid for the service, although she couldn't make the trip to the funeral. They sang a few songs, but I couldn't bring myself to join in. The girl beside me had a lovely singing voice and carried the whole pew. Everyone else just seemed to mumble along. I stood and was blankly looking forward towards the front of the church just thinking, relaxing, still a little stoned. I lit up a smoke, but the Silk Spectre glared so I put it out on my shoe.

After the second hymn, the priest introduced me as 'Joe's only son' and called me up to speak. I could tell that Silk Spectre was shocked and I shot her a soft smile. I ran my hand through my floppy hair as I walked between the rows, looking at the ten or so people that had gathered and then glancing at my mother who was smoking a long cigarette and scratching at her arm.

Bloody junky, I thought. I stood for a moment longer. Someone coughed. There was always a cougher at things like this—someone to break the long, uncomfortable silences. I stood for a moment longer. My mother made a gesture to me as if to get on with it. I opened my mouth, and the words flowed.

"People have told me that my father Joe was a good man. I could never really hold a candle to that. We didn't have anything more in common than strangers on the street. My father would keep the attention of everyone in the room. When he stood, people around him stood. When he smoked, so would everyone else. The man I knew had a lot of vices. And, although I only learned of his death today, I'm sure it was one of those vices that got him. I know this service is a Catholic one; for that, I have a few problems." I looked over at the priest whose jaw dropped just a little. "God is in every man, not necessarily in religion. I came to that conclusion as I walked the streets this morning. In every man there is God, he is easier to find in some than in others, but he is there—and he was in my father, to a small extent. He brought me into this world; what can you really say about someone that gave you life? My father is my temple, my teacher, and my god. But if you were to beat me with a stick until I bleed, I could not tell you one decent thing I remember of him—I spent the morning trying to, trust me. He made me who I am. He is my father, so I'm entirely grateful for him and I will spend maybe the rest of my life trying to learn from him and not feed the demons inside of me as he did. I don't know what he would have wanted me to do because we never talked about such things, but I'm sure I will be better. Better than his shortcomings and his failures. His life was the example of the wrong life and the life he taught me not to lead, and that is how I will remember him: showing me the ways not to be. So that his example will bring out the best in me and I'm sure it will for all of you here walking the same path as him. Thank you."

And that was it. I didn't look at any of the stares I received as I walked back. I'd spoken the truth as I saw it. I sat at the back as one of his friends got up to speak; the man glared at me as if I had ruined his whole talk. Clearly, he was going to reminisce about the good times as he should. I decided it was time to leave. Throwing on my coat, I walked out of the church where I stood briefly and lit a smoke. There were tears in my eyes. It was a strange feeling, and part of me wished I could have just told that to the old man—told him everything I'd just said.

I walked over to my bike.

"Hey, wait!" I looked up and saw Silk Spectre running towards me. "Nice speech, I guess."

"Thanks."

"Where are you heading?"

"To get properly messed up." I smiled.

"So, you aren't living what you preached?"

"Maybe one day."

"Pity," she said. "Would you want to grab a drink later? I could shed a little light on what I knew of Joe."

"Well, how about dinner?"

"Sure! I know a good place downtown. Vietnamese okay?"

"I love a good pho," I said.

"Okay, meet me at the corner of 105th Street and 107th Ave. at six."

"Okay, Silk. I'll be there."

"Good."

CHAPTER 14

As I rode my cycle through range roads, I was careful to avoid major highways as my record wasn't exactly clean; I had bad luck with cops. I thought about how one person can perceive a situation differently from everyone else. Any change to the world, good or bad, came from people who just were different in perspective. It pays to be different. It might not pay in one's lifetime, but that little bit of oddity—how someone acted, how bad they may have been before—really had no bearing if someone was worth it now, in the present. The present representation of a person was all that mattered. Not how they acted in the past and not how they were going to act in the future. Yet we all hold on so tightly to that previous representation and even refuse the present. There are moments in human interaction where words flow and the moment is right. Maybe she caught my father at a time like that. A moment of clarity; a moment where she saw something in him. That thought of seeing God in people was flooding my mind again. That was the theme, and it seemed to be playing out over and over on this day.

I pulled up at my uncle's quiet farm outside the city, close to the church. That, I didn't understand; what was so great about living in the past? No one farmed anymore. Soon, it would all be 100% efficient machines. Machines that would just turn the grain into perfect loaves of bread as they sucked it straight up into their combines. It was a dying skill set. My uncle was a dairy farmer by day. The kind of job where you don't get any time off not like the lazy grain guys who—definitely, in Alberta—get the vast majority of the year off, as he would always say. Having a dairy farm is the kind of job where you would need lots of children to help with the never-ending chores. That was my opinion of the job and, mind you, me repeating it had led to one or two cowboy bar fights. My uncle's wife left him and took the four children. Something about him middle-manning drugs by hiding large shipments so they could be distributed for the entire city of Edmonton and surrounding areas. That was why I was here. Because last night I wanted to show dangerous people a good time. I wondered how much money they had at the start of the night. What I had made off with must have been for the 'heads tonight at The Bronx.

I pulled up to the large farmhouse. It looked a little like a classy southern plantation farm. The place worked better than a shipping yard. Even though he had only about fifty cattle, my uncle was superb at cooking the books. He was sitting on the front porch with some water simmering on a burner when I walked up. The man didn't have the look of a dealer. He was good to me, even though I didn't know about him until I was deep into Edmonton's drug scene; he would have nothing to do with my parents.

He was in his forties and still fit. He wore a Canadian tuxedo, was clean-shaven, and loved his shitty straw hat. He was the real deal. I sat down beside him as he tended to the water.

"You're back," he said. "I thought you would have left town after last night."

"Should I have? I don't really recall."

"You were so fucked up last night. You thought it would be a good idea to take a roofie; the other guys you were with didn't believe you when you told them it was just like getting wasted and to stop being pussies."

"That explains why I can't remember much."

"Well, lucky for you, I have just the cure," he said.

"And what might that be?" I asked, lighting a smoke and realizing the first pack was starting to run low.

He looked at me and smiled. "I heard about the funeral... Did you go? I couldn't bear see that group of miserable junkies that your father hung out with."

"Yeah, I went and spoke. On my mother's request. Bet she regretted it a bit."

"I see. Well, let us have our own little wake party then."

"I was hoping we could talk about last night."

He jumped straight into it. "Yes, you're in trouble with a dangerous group of people." He poured the contents of the boiling pot into a kettle and brought it over to the table and set it down, then pulled out two steel blue cups covered with small white dots. He placed one in front of me, filled with the mystery liquid.

"What is this? English breakfast?" I asked.

"Nope. Only the finest, straight from Vancouver Island. Delivered this morning."

"You're testing product on me? This is a first."

"Like I said, it's a wake."

"How strong are we talking? I have a hot date later... Three of them, actually."

"Okay, okay. Just one cup for you. I'll let mine steep a little longer. It's a nice day out here, don't you think?"

"You got a joint? Can't wait around all day for this to kick in."

"Sure." He pulled a silver cigarette case from his jean jacket and lit a spliff from it.

I took a small sip. "You're sure I'll still be my usual charming self; I won't be completely knocked out?"

"Son, would I lie to you?" he said after taking a long drag, thick smoke leaving his lips.

I looked up and laughed.

"I need to know what you can tell me about last night. Who is after me? I have a pretty good idea, but I'm still unsure who was even here." My mind was already starting to empty. Part of me drifted through space; I don't think I fully ever got that part back.

He looked back at me. "Well, for starters…"

CHAPTER 15

The lines in the world began to mould together. The fields swayed as if water commanded them. My uncle was talking to me, but the words failed to reach my ears. Life was perfect. I would catch the odd word like big buyers, new clients, bikers, big shipment, and cash box, but he sounded distant. The words wouldn't stay with me long as I watched the fields ripple in the wind. Suddenly I liked the country very much. I could hear the sounds of distant birds, the sound of their wings breaking the air. I could hear cows chewing. All the sounds amplified, flooding my ears, as I just stared out at the horizon. This was how life was meant to be viewed.

"Hey, are you listening to me?"

"Umm, yeah," I replied as my focus turned to him.

"So those guys you were with said they wanted to move product through me. You pulled me aside and told me you had a grand joke to pull on them."

"I did? What was the joke?"

"You said you were going to rip them off. They had cash that they needed to pay off the skinheads for a deal that went wrong. They got the cash from a hit they pulled off. You kept saying it would be so funny if that money disappeared. A grand joke, you kept saying: pit the gangs against the 'heads."

I tried to listen, but the fields—the long, empty fields—held my gaze.

"I see."

"Did you do it? Are you being hunted by these men?"

"Yeah, I think so..."

"Listen. They *will* kill you. This is serious. You have to use that money to leave town."

"Uncle, I have a plan. Just wait and see."

"You have to go right now! Is the money in town?

You should wait here until it's dark, get the money, and take off west. I know people in the interior that could help you hide out."

"I wish I could, but I have a hot date with Silk Spectre."

"What? This is no time for dumb comic book jokes. You're in trouble. The cops came out here last night and you hopped in a car with some bikers, and then they chased... Cops must have thought you were trespassing on my land."

"What would give them that idea?"

"I don't know, man. I live on a farm, but I still have neighbours."

"They called the cops on us?"

"Must have..."

He pulled out a cigarette and started smoking, passing one to me. I lit it and looked at him. His face—the lines on it, they flowed as he talked just like the fields. Just like the earth.

"And now that you've pulled off the joke, get out of the city. It's too hot for you here."

"I'm not scared of those pussy skinheads."

"So what are you going to do? You're really up shit creek."

"I'm going to do what I've always done: go out to The Bronx tonight, maybe get on stage with the band, hop into the mosh pit—have a good time."

"Listen, I care about you. Stop screwing around and get out of the city. Where's the money? How much was it?"

"It was, like, ten thousand dollars."

"And where have you hidden it?"

"I gave it away,"

"What!?"

"Yeah. I gave it to a homeless man."

"Have you fucking lost it?"

"Maybe, man. What is a conscience anyways? What does it mean? When can you tell it's gone?" He rolled his eyes and cursed, but I quickly threw in. "I'm a man to be watched. I have many cards up my sleeves."

"Just stop, okay?"

Then we just sat and looked out at the road that approached the house. He picked up his porch guitar and strummed. The sound carried. Maybe it just took the tea to see the flow that was always there. Maybe when life fell out of flow, you just had to stop and take it back.

CHAPTER 16

When I found my uncle's voice again, it was as if the words were in my mind.

"I have something important to tell you," my uncle said. "I never thought I would have to; it has to do with a sort of inheritance your father left for you."

"Why would he leave anything for me? The man hated me."

"Maybe on the surface. Maybe only after he realized you were turning into him."

"I will never become like that man."

"Listen, you didn't know him when he was your age... Well, you two are alike. Both into jokes. Both into dangerous jokes."

"What did he do?"

My uncle looked out at the fields. You could hear the cows and the birds, and I thought once again about being able to see the flow.

"When he had you, he wanted you to live extremely well and he figured you were the greatest gift for him—that you would do great things."

I thought about this. It was as if he was talking about completely different people.

"He wanted you to have money and live a good life. Him and four of his buddies, who all had kids around the same time, all wanted their children to get out of the shit. But they were all junkies, and they realized that their addictions would destroy them. So, when they heard about a big deal going down in BC— something Triad related—they re-routed the money for themselves and hid it away in Arizona, burying it under a tight pack until the heat died down.

I stared at the man, trying to grasp what he said. I

knew Joe was capable of such things, but for the money to go to me? It didn't make any sense.

"Your father planned the whole thing, and now there is only one guy left who knows where the money is. Two of the kids died in a drunk-driving crash a few years back and their fathers were killed in a gang hit last night. It's been all over the news."

Must have been the hit I stole the money from.

"Someone let the whole story slip to some desperate bikers."

"How did my father die?" I asked. I had just assumed it was something drug-related.

"He shot himself."

I looked down at the ground.

"Oh..."

"The fourth man on the deal went crazy and no one really knows where he is."

"Then why are you telling me this?" I asked, slowly realizing how learning about some money my father stole that nobody could find made little difference to my life.

"I don't know. I just thought I would try and help you. Let you know how much the man cared about you. Imagine a junkie with all that money putting it away for his family without ever touching it. Now if you can track down the fourth guy then the money will be at least locatable. You can grow up, you can become better, and you can do great things. I only tell you because I wanted you to know that Joe did do something for you. Something big."

Whatever was in the tea began to wear off. The lines in the world slowly returned. All that was left was a feeling that I had seen the other side and now I was coming back. The experience was unlike any drug I had ever used; the snap of coming back was very subtle, if there was one at all.

"I never knew the man. I would have never guessed he was capable of doing such things. All the hard times we went through. All the evictions, all the past-due notices. I just don't understand why if he had all that money."

"He was complicated. He would do things that made no sense to help people, even though he was a junkie."

I lit up a smoke and thought about a cash box hidden somewhere in Arizona—and about the suicide. Then I thought about the heat I had brought about on myself the previous night. Now, more importantly than ever, I needed to find this fourth guy who might be able to help me. But where to even start?

"This will be your journey." He looked at me. "Come help me milk some cows before you go. I have to make a living, you know."

I smiled "Right. Dairy farming is like a tenth of your living."

He ignored this. "Come on now, stop being so damn lazy."

CHAPTER 17

"So who was Joe? I mean, around me he was almost always either drunk or on something. I knew him only as that guy that was supposed to matter, but didn't really. That is how I viewed him."

"Now you want to know, eh? After the smoke has cleared?"

"Yeah man, I'm feeling good. Now I kind of have something like a treasure hunt to spend the rest of my life on. I should learn more about him, I guess."

"That makes two of us," my uncle said, as he brought me into the milking room and lined the cows up.

It takes cows a while to get used to a routine, but then they fall into place like they have no thoughts other than to drink, eat, give birth, and be milked. Human beings are also meant to live in a cosmic routine, and the course of everyone's life was just as predictable. That's how the higher power intended it to be: just a blissful flow. Everyone's life is just a different array of eating, drinking and giving birth. Not my life, though, and also not the life of my father, Joe.

"Your father's mind was great, but he didn't want all those thoughts—so he killed them. Killed them with the kind of drugs you're getting into. He felt the pains of his genius his whole life; intelligence was something he wanted nothing to do with. It was the wrong time for him. Wrong social class. Left him on the path of self-destruction, as it were."

I nodded, watching my uncle attach the suction lines to the cows. *I knew my father*, I thought. But the more I heard, the less I understood. I didn't feel sorry about the speech because that was who he was to me. If our places had been reversed, I'm sure he would have just gone on about what a disappointment I was.

"Well shit, man," I said. The effects of the drugs were still holding points in my mind and I was finding it hard to focus on the words being said.

"So, tell me: now that you know about the money, what would you do if you found it?"

"I'd probably go down to Argentina, buy a place by the beach, read books, smoke weed and cigarettes, and drink coffee until the end of my days."

"Sounds like a plan. You should consider starting a small farm. Do you know why I keep the animals? Why I work every day when my other business ventures pay the bills three times over?"

I shook my head.

"Because you can party all you want. You can live the good life. But at the end of the day, all you are is just like one of these cows. Routine is the cornerstone of all life. You ought to know that by now—and if you don't, it is damn time you figured it out. The partying and the drugs become your routine, and then one day your mind will go and all the coffee and cigarettes won't take that edge off."

I lit a smoke and looked up at him. He levelled at my eyes. This man, his life, my life, and all the consequences to come on this day were all too entwined. The 'heads would be after me soon, the bikers would also be gunning for me, and now I had to find this crazy man and complete this crazy joke.

"Chaos is the only way to live. It is the answer. Do you want me to do nothing but mindless work until I die with the only definition of my life being that routine? Chaos is life. The only time you are alive is in moments of chaos. People look at you and all they see you as is a farmer, yet your other life gives you the chaos you crave. You will understand that one day. When the drug shipments take over and the cows go hungry, chaos is the state where people can be truly free."

It was time I left. I surprisingly hadn't burned through too much time; the tea and weed slowed things down quite a bit. My uncle nodded, but his smile faded. I had figured out the chaos. And what was more, I could control it.

CHAPTER 18

I walked down the path from the farm house to my motorcycle, still waiting for the effects of the comedown. I sat on top of the bike—the bike I had stolen from the man I was learning more and more about. I had thought all I would get from him was this bike, but now it seemed there was all that money, too. Only one man knew where the money was. I had no name or address, but I would find him. The more pressing problem was the stolen money. Hopefully, I could pit the 'heads against the bikers and slide away so they would forget the reason behind the fight; a real win-win that would allow me to search in relative peace. As I started to ride back towards the city, I still saw the lines—a kind of wholeness with the universe, which I was but a small piece of. I couldn't decide if I was going to make a big splash, or if coffee and cigarettes on a beach would be the extent of the impact I was to make. All I knew was that the fields with their crops blown by the wind were reflective of the patterns of life that hold it all together. Chaos was harder to find on the farms—more difficult to hold up. The city was my chaos. The night I was riding towards was my storm. This cash box was all that mattered; it was my father's gift and my ticket to freedom from this life. To start my own fire, sit back and watch the world burn.

The bike purred as I slowed into a lower gear, lighting a smoke at an intersection. I thought more about the events that would happen tonight and the dismantling of the machine. I headed down Baseline into Capilano. There was a small pool hall just west of Capilano Mall; I figured, before I went calling on the guitarist, I would hustle up some cash shooting pool. I had almost all the pieces in place, but now I didn't care how I had ended up in that ditch. 'You are where you are.' The guitarist may know, but it didn't seem to matter anymore. I pulled up in front of the pool hall and stopped in at the tobacconist next to it.

"What can I get for you?" asked a Korean lady with slender eyes behind large-framed glasses.

"Give me a pack of cloves and a pack of Player's Special Blend." She gathered the cigarettes and put them on the counter.

"Anything else?"

"Yeah, give me a copy of the Sun." I wanted to read up on yesterday's gang hit.

"Everyone's afraid these days," she said as I handed her some bills.

"And why is that?" I asked.

"I serve so many skinheads and racists that hang around that pool hall. When I left my country, I came looking for a good life. A Canadian dream, if you would. Think I was welcomed over here? Think I was appreciated? No. White people like you hate everything and everyone."

"Hey, lady, don't lump me in with those fascist bastards. I'm on your side. This is Canada, the greatest country in the world, and you should make the most of it." I smiled at her. "Don't judge me for looking like those goddamn 'heads. Not everyone you see that dresses this way hates you for being here. Hell, the most racist people in Alberta aren't open about it like those 'heads are. The ones that you have to watch out for are the ones within white picket fences. The ones that pay their taxes on time. They will abandon you in a heartbeat. All those skinheads want is the next high. Those blue-collared workers that stick to themselves and their families are the ones with buried hate. You're smarter, work harder, and you might end up with their job—and that terrifies them."

She looked down, "Regardless, I always keep one of these handy." She pulled out a shotgun out from behind the counter, showing a broad smile.

"Holy shit, Lady!" I said slowly backing away, laughing nervously, "Listen. Anyone tries to rip you off, don't think twice." I stumbled out the door into the parking lot. Canadian dream. That's damn straight. I finished a smoke and walked to the entrance of the pool hall hoping to turn my last twenty dollars into a hundred so I could buy Silk Spectre some eats and have enough for a few bottles later with Mike and Matt.

CHAPTER 19

I walked into the pool hall. It was a slow time of day. The hall had about twenty tables, so it was a good place to hang out or hide. It didn't take me to much time to find out who my 'mark' was: a skinny man, about thirty or so, with thick glasses and almost no hair except for a few still-clinging tufts on the side. I went to the bar and watched him. He seemed to be on a hot streak and was cockily collecting money from all his friends. I ordered a beer and admired his skill. He was a good player. He probably had a family at home that he was escaping from. Having a family was the supposed to be the Holy Grail, and yet so many sought refuge from that family. Even cave men probably snuck off in the night to sit with their buddies and grunt away. In this case, grunting was replaced with betting.

I skimmed the paper; there was a picture of one of the men suspected to be in the shooting. Of course, it was the old biker. *Whatever,* I thought. *Doesn't matter now.* I ran my hand down my face and put on my best drunk and cocky look then approached the group.

"Hey, guys," I said. The mark looked over at me from the game.

"How's she going?" he asked, not expressing any interest.

"Oh, she's going. How about me and you play the next game? Twenty dollars."

"You seem a little drunk, kid. I'm just here with my buddies. Not out to take anyone else's money."

"Listen, man. I'm feeling hot," I said as I chalked a cue. "Do you have some place to be? Family? I'm sure you could use another game away from them. It's twenty easy dollars if you're so confident."

He looked at me and smiled, sipped his beer, and smoked. I followed suit, struggling with the lighter a little.

"Alright, milk and eggs money. Sure." The game in front of us was almost ending.

"Yeah. Milk, and eggs... For me, another beer or two; had kind of an interesting day."

"Oh yeah? What kind of problems could you have? What in the world could go wrong in your life?" he countered.

"Hey, man. A lot can. My boss treating me like garbage and sending me home early. Now I just want to get drunk, but payday isn't until the 15th and all I have is a little money. Need to make some more."

"You would have better chances on the horses then beating me at pool—especially today. But alright." His two buddies finished up their game of eight-ball, and the man beside me put out his smoke.

"Hey, we're going to grab some food at the bar," the oldest of the three said, "Ralph. You coming with, or are you going to roll on this punk?"

"I'm going to play him one quick game. I'll meet

you guys at the bar in fifteen."

They left Ralph and me to play a few games. I was still playing the drunk and put my twenty on the table. Ralph followed suit.

"What's your name, kid?"

"Clark Kent. I'll rack. Eight-ball work for you?"

"You know, we just finished a game of eight-ball. How about nine instead?"

"Whatever you say, Ralph."

Still acting a bit drunk, I racked the balls then downed half of my beer in one go. I perched myself on a stool as Ralph set up to break.

With a loud snap, the balls broke—sinking the three, the five, and the one, but missing the two. Ralph's turn ended there. He grinned at me as he chalked his cue.

"So where do you work?" he asked. I looked up at him as I lined up to sink the two, but missed.

"I work at a gas station on 50th Street." This was my standard story whenever anyone asked me where I worked because it was kind of untraceable and easy to forget. "And you?" I asked back as he sunk the two and then the four. I watched the table and noticed that the nine was in good shape to sink off the seven.

"I'm in school, studying for Masters in Psychology."

"Study of the mind, eh? I wouldn't want to open up that bag of cats myself."

"Yeah, lots of people say that." He sunk the six and lined up the seven.

"So, do you love your mother or something? That

Freudian garbage?" The comment caught him off guard a bit, so he missed the seven trying to bank it.

He looked over at me "You should read more philosophy; Nietzsche, in particular, is more my speed. I'm sure his thoughts are more your style as well. Freud doesn't really do anything for me."

"Nietzsche? The one with the Superman-Hitler-propaganda?" I said as I hit the seven into the nine, knocking it in and winning the game. I smiled as I looked up at him.

"Good game," he said. I could tell that he was pissed off, and just like I expected: "Why don't we keep it going? Forty dollars, best of three. You've got some skill. And by the way, that was Nietzsche's sister; she was the Nazi and twisted her brother's words after taking him into her care. The man himself wanted nothing to do with the Germans or the direction they were going and said it many times."

"Yeah. Sure, sure." The table was racked again,

"I'll order us another round," Ralph said as he called the waitress over. Out of the corner of my eye, I saw two motorcycles pull up outside. I recognized them instantly. They stood outside behind the tinted pool hall windows arguing in hushed voices.

What a painfully small world.

CHAPTER 20

Ralph won the next game quickly since we didn't talk. He racked the balls for the second game.

"You seem to have some worldly knowledge," he said.

"I know enough to get by—to hold my own in conversation."

Ralph smiled at this. "I see... You got a girl? Got an old lady at home?"

"No," I said back. "Met a girl today going out for dinner. We'll see what happens. And you?"

He lined up another shot. "Yeah, I've got a wife and two kids at home."

"I always figured I would be happier just drinking and sleeping around than having a wife and children."

He won the second game, but I objected before he could reach out his hand for the money. "How about we double it one more time? No money changes hands yet—best of five for $80."

He looked me up and down. "Alright. You know, you'll learn that having kids and a wife is the course of life on this planet. When you get older, you kind of pity people without them. That is the ultimate philosophy. Even gang runners or hard men are envious of the family life. They crave it because somewhere along the way it's just what needs to happen. It's the hormones. People are always confused about the meaning of life, but it's always right in front of them. If aliens were to come to our planet, they would give one look around and just say 'Hey, that's the human purpose.'"

He said all of this as he won the first and second game. He was racking up for the third and what would be the final game—for which I had no money to pay—when I responded:

"I would have to disagree with you. Having a higher education in psychology shows that you have settled on these thoughts. The things you learn in school, from what I know, would not steer you towards this conclusion. This is what you tell yourself to make it work. This is your cop-out. You said this is the be-all-end-all of the human existence. Instead of challenging meaning and purpose you spend your time at the bars with your buddies not wearing your ring—which to me shows that this conclusion has crippled you. I can tell that you are not a man of religion. I have developed quite the eye for watching out for that type and so your life is flawed because if you were a man of the old god, you would not be a man of challenging thought. You would not then conform to the most aged intention of religion. Basically: have a family, go to church, and stop questioning. You have become a man of faith without a god and you don't even realize it."

I said all of this as I won the next two games. Our next game would determine who takes the money. Ralph lit up a smoke and sat down. I looked across the table watching him mutter as I smoked as well.

"And you? The free bird? You'll be hiding behind a shield your whole life if you don't find happiness other than a fleeting glimpse of it through the bottom of a bottle."

I looked at him right in the eyes: "We're both right, Ralph. And it is in our act of arguing that makes it so. Don't stop thinking, Ralph, and don't stop arguing." I said as I set myself to break the well-organized chaos— the cluster of life that is the game of pool.

CHAPTER 21

Out of the corner of my eye, I saw the two bikers were still outside. It looked like their conversation was getting more and more heated. I turned back to the game. It was definitely the bikers from the night before. There was a loud snap as the balls scattered across the table. I sunk the eight, the three, and four with ease—

and then I sunk the one. Ralph took aim, but I knew he was deflated. He sunk the two and the five. When I looked outside again, the bikers had left and had now seated themselves at the bar with their backs to us.

"You know," Ralph said, "your argument isn't half bad, but you've forgotten one imperative aspect of life on this planet."

"And what might that be?" I lit another smoke.

"Love."

"Love? Fuck off."

"The type of life you want to lead in thought—in searching for the meaning—leaves out love. And for that, you will never have full answers."

"But you speak of the love between people, not the love of a good cup of coffee or the love of riding a motorcycle on a hot summer day. Love is oneness with the world. I feel that people only give their love to one another without giving much recognition to the love that one can find all by himself on this planet. That you say purpose is only with the love of another—I have you beat, Ralph. You may be smarter than me, but you have just settled on the answer that fits your picture just like everyone else. You found love and, in it, you stopped thinking about what other answers are really out there. With that, I would like my eighty dollars. This game is mine." I could still feel the tea and it gave my words such charm.

I looked up at him as I lined up the shot for the win. He grinned as I sunk the ball with an arrogant strike.

"How can you tell me that you didn't fall in love just a little bit as I made that shot and won the game?"

"You will realize, sooner than later, that what you're after in life will not find you—and will, in fact, provide the catalyst for quite another life. And that—"

"That was nicely put." I interrupted him, suddenly sensing an urgency. The bikers had been looking at me too intensely.

"I guess so," he said.

I reached out and took the money off the table. It would provide for a good night of drugs, sex, and liquor as all greenbacks did. In the corner of my eye, I realized that the biker was walking towards us.

"Where's the fucking money!?" He said as the bar quieted. I quickly stuffed the winnings in my pocket.

"Hey, man, the money's coming."

"Yeah, you shit! When we threw you out of the car during the chase, we thought you'd died. But if you don't give us the money this second—" Ralph backed away and slowly left the pool table, leaving me to fend for myself—rightly so.

I held the pool cue in one hand and my empty pint glass in the other as the other younger biker approached me from the left side.

"Listen, the money's at my place. I'll bring it to The Bronx tonight. Everything is all good."

"You'll give us the money now!"

Out of the corner of my eye I saw a bottle fly through the air and hit the biker in the back of the head. When his partner turned, I hit him across the face with a pint glass, breaking his nose. The first guy then pulled his knife, but I split the cue over his head. I quickly hopped over the pool table and ran out of the bar. The two bikers were left behind holding their heads in pain. Ralph was standing at the bar, smoking and looking only slightly disconcerted. He raised his glass. I bolted out of the door and ran to my bike. Starting it, I jetted out of the parking lot towards Whyte Ave. I smiled; Ralph had one hell of an arm.

CHAPTER 22

Now I knew how high the stakes were. I revved through the traffic circle going almost sixty, then down the hill into the valley where the annual Folk Fest is held; a good drinking time. I had gone ever since I was eleven and it was the only family outing we did every year. My parents were always sneaking in drugs. They did love each other in their way; it had always crossed my mind, but now it brought tears to my eyes.

My thoughts flashed back to the bar: those guys wanted their money bad. But life is for the risky, and getting chased out of bars is all part of the risky routine. The sun was still high in the sky. It stays high all summer, driving the vibe in Edmonton upwards. Then it dips low in the winter again, taking everyone's moods with it.

I reflected with disbelief on the bar fight I had just escaped. Shaking my head to myself, I wondered when the tea would wear off.

I was on my way back to Whyte Avenue, still racing away, and beginning to truly feel the weight of the day on my shoulders. I needed an upper—maybe a few. But then, was that really what I needed? I thought of what my uncle had to say about the cash box. Was that all real? The places I'd go with that money. Crossing over the North Saskatchewan River onto the High Level Bridge, I weaved through traffic yet again. I thought of Ralph with his be-all-end-all life. What a guy. How could an educated man reach such empty conclusions? Mind you, the structure of school and learning is so flawed; the systems on which you are graded. And why do the marks exist, even? To determine who is smart? Or maybe just whose minds are set forward. The guy looking out the window finding things outside the classroom and looking out at the world—maybe he is the smartest. If he relents, accepting the suit-and-tie gig that all his peers are striving for, he would be a drone. And never have his day or his parade. He'd be stuck looking out windows forever, wanting more.

I kept on driving south down 109th Street a little ways past Whyte Ave. I could hear music as soon as I pulled up to the guitarist's house. In my mind, the truly gifted are the musicians. Musicians are always looking; musicians are always talking. I checked over my shoulder to see if the bikers had followed me. I was pretty confident that they hadn't but, just in case, I brought my bike around to the back of the pink stucco house. Through the basement window, I could see the guitarist as he played away. I banged on the glass to get his attention. *Shit*, I thought. *I should have grabbed some beer.* He waved his hand for me to come in. He had long blond hair, a matching goatee, and was playing shirtless. It must have been close to five. *Is that possible?* I wondered, trying to count the hours that had gone by. So much time seemed to have passed but, yet again, not a moment of the day had been wasted. Not a breath.

Walking down the unlit stairs and lighting a smoke, I thought again about needing an upper as I remembered the date with Silk Spectre. I was beginning, very slowly, to think that I maybe didn't need uppers in my life. After all, life seemed to be giving me some great high.

My mind was scattered in all corners as I opened the door and stared in at the main room. This was a house of the revolution.

CHAPTER 23

"Hey, how's she going?" He asked as I sat on the second-hand couch and sparked up one of his joints.

"Not too bad. You know, everyday struggles."

"That was one crazy party last night. Thanks for the invite to the farm; your uncle always has the finest selection."

"Yeah, man. No worries... I'm in pretty deep, aren't I?"

"Yeah, I think about leaving town on the regular—but for you, I'm thinking you should really leave. Like after you get good and stoned. Fancy anything a bit harder?"

"Nah, man. This is hitting the spot. Give up every drug but weed, isn't that what our fathers always said?"

He laughed, "Like those guys could give up everything but weed. That's the dream. You were ripping on your old man pretty hard last night, you remember? You, uh, got pretty emotional."

"Doesn't sound like me. Maybe I sensed something. You know, that third-eye shit."

"I hear you can buy that in South America."

"Yeah, I've heard that too... But man, my dad was buried today."

"Fuck! Are you serious?"

"Yeah, I gave a speech and everything."

"Shit... Did you mention that cherry of a story when your old man smacked me across the face for talking back to him?"

I laughed as I walked over to the mini-fridge and grabbed a beer. "I wasn't very nice in front of his groupies and my mother; she's a train wreck, man. There was this girl there, though, and apparently I have a date with her tonight, which is pretty wild. She said she knew my father. Well, from stories at least."

"Strange."

"Yeah, man, you knew Joe like I did, but I've just been learning some new things about the guy."

I knew I couldn't tell him about the cash box. It looked like his addictions were creeping up on him. I wondered how aware of that he was.

"You know what would give a little more to the exploration on this day? A little smack. You in?"

"Nah... I'm good."

"Suit yourself," he said as he heated a spoon and readied a syringe.

"Come on, why do you do that to yourself? Watching you self-destruct kills me. Using a fucking needle is so hurting, man."

"Wow, buddy. Chill out. What's with you today? Even last night it was like you're losing yourself. It's like you've forgotten where we come from. 'Following in the footsteps of our partying fathers.' That's a quote from you. Remember that, because *this* is the party," he gestured with the syringe.

"Fuck."

"Hey, man, even just last night you would have been fine with this. You would have taken in on it. What's happening to you?"

"Maybe I'm just starting to realize the traps in this world, how you get screwed, and addiction is the worst way. The worst hook. Get addicted to money or women or anything else instead and kill yourself with smoking nice and slow. At least she takes the edge off."

"*This* takes the edge off, man."

"It's not the same. There are so many ways to fuck up your life. To miss the mark. That's what our fathers did: they missed the mark by a fucking long shot. We used to joke about following in their footsteps. I never really wanted that shit. Do you have anything you want? Any goals? *Any* fucking thing?"

"Hey, man! What's with you? You're not your usual chill self. What's happened to you today?"

My voice was starting to crack. "Maybe it's just a moment of clarity that has been a lifetime in the making. Maybe I have just seen the blur in the lines."

"Blur in the lines? What the shit are you talking about?"

"What I'm talking about... There are lines—lines in life you're supposed to walk down. Do this. Stay in line. Falling out of line is just another played-out path. You're just becoming a messed-up junkie wasting your talent by flirting with death." I looked away from him as I spoke. I was starting to choke up.

"You wrote the book on flirting with death,

buddy." As he said this, I could see he was getting anxious. I thought of our fathers at that moment. Why was everything pissing me off? My best friend had had this habit for a while now, and it never bothered me like this before. I couldn't comprehend my emotions.

"There's flirting with death, and then there's death itself, man," I said as I stood up and walked towards the door then turned and looked back, leaving the full beer on the foot of the stairs. His eyes were wide as he looked at me in disbelief, trying to grasp words. Trying to figure it out. My whole chill existence seemed to be ruptured. The funeral, the mushrooms tea, or whatever it was, and all the smokes brought me to this point.

"Hey," he finally said, "I'm opening tonight at The Bronx. You going to come?"

I started to put on my leather jacket as I lit a smoke, feeling the empty-headedness that came with the weed but trying to refocus my thoughts in vain. I was operating on instincts now. I had the date with Silk Spectre next. "Bro, you know I wouldn't miss," I said without turning and walked back up the dimly lit stairway and out of his apartment. Something made me look into his window and I saw him put the needle into his arm. "Death itself," I repeated in a whisper.

CHAPTER 24

It was almost time to meet Silk Spectre. I was still thinking about the guitarist shooting up. Sure, I had my addictions, but heroin was a different breed—it was at the top of the FDA-approved drug pyramid for a reason. I smoked as I rode my bike back downtown. The joke was the point. It was all about having the best joke. My father was a jokester; that was the part of him I never knew. Now, only in death was it becoming clear that my disdain wasn't completely merited. Sure, we would have never got along. But the stunt he pulled! He would have been proud of me pissing off the 'heads this evening, and I thought about it a little more as I rode. Driving downtown, I thought of the Punk community I was part of. How it flowed and moved like the fields. The drugs and the gangs never really bothered me. I always figured it gave pace to life. It gave the excitement: taking edges off, putting edges on—that was the way it was. I had some time to kill before my big date, where hopefully the Silk Spectre would give me a little bit more knowledge on Joe.

I decided to sit on a bench overlooking the river and have a few smokes. The sun seemed to barely move on these deep days of summer. *Maybe the community is wrong*, I thought. But that couldn't be. The community, my crew—that was my life. The more I learned as the day unfolded, the more I fought to learn, staring out into the full display of green that filled the valley below. Lighting another smoke, I thought back again to the time my old man pushed me into the lake. I would often joke that I would wind up like him, but now the guitarist was really ending up like his father. And it wasn't funny. I had one more smoke before I headed to the pho house to meet the Silk Spectre.

I was there first, so I sat down and ordered some salad rolls. I started looking at the people outside the window: businessmen in their individual bubbles walking about like each person had a dome around their heads that stopped them from actually seeing the world. I sensed that those shutters were just going to get smaller as the world advances. Soon the bubble would become so tight and conversation and interaction would become so rare that some wouldn't even be able to handle anything outside of their sphere. This would happen soon. It seemed that technology was advancing exponentially. I thought back on how far it had come since early the '80s, when I didn't believe that it could progress that much more. I hadn't conceived of these bubbles, this empty type of life that everyone was beginning to lead. Surely, nothing so drastic was going to happen in my lifetime. But then, there is a new century coming up. And if I lived to see it, I was sure it would bring about the end of everyone's social life. All people would see would be the inside of their bubble where they would grin and smirk. Their whole existence would consist of smirking and grinning.

I watched a homeless woman pushing her cart. She looked good and haggard. At first glance she looked just a few steps away from death, but I could see in her eyes that she was very much alive. Seeing her next to a businessman on one of those expensive portable phones provided an ironic comparison.

My salad rolls arrived, big pieces of shrimp with a peanut sauce. They looked like the best I had seen. Maybe the Silk Spectre did know her stuff. I devoured them and then order a coffee with some whisky in it. A bit of an empty gesture on my part but, to my surprise, the waitress responded warmly and brought it right over.

This was living: dining by yourself with just a hint that you might be stood up by your date, but still sitting with the confidence that all you need is the newspaper. I didn't even need the paper anymore; I had the entire world. After a while lost in my head, I saw the Silk Spectre arriving in a camper van. She parked it so swiftly and smoothly between a Beetle and a motorcycle. I wondered if our lives shared a timeline and kinship. With those parking skills and that in mind, she must have stolen the van from her father. Between the weed and that damn tea, I had almost forgotten how attractive she was. Seeing me in the window, she smiled and waved then sat right down and ordered a coffee with whisky.

CHAPTER 25

Silk just stared, forcing me to start the conversation.

"So how was the rest of your afternoon? I like your van. Bet you shag a lot of guys in that rolling bed."

"Guys? I've found girls to be much more interesting of late." She smiled and ordered: two orders of the number six—tripe and brisket pho.

"So, Silk, you said you have some relation to Joe. Usually that wouldn't interest me, but today has been a little more than eye-opening."

"That's it? I'm not too sure about you; let's get to know each other first. Do you ever do up that Mohawk?"

"Only girls style their hair. I thought I told you that. Or wait, must have been... someone else. Well, where to start? I'm a revolutionary. The world is my battlefield, society the criminal. Blue collar, white collar: I'm striving to free them all."

"That sounds like the biggest load of bullshit I have ever heard. What you're telling me is that you're a deadbeat, most likely a drug addict, who has no job and no purpose."

I leant back in my chair. "Shit, Silk. You know, you're kind of right. What's your story, then?"

"Myself? I'm a masked vigilante, following in the

footsteps of my mother, Miss Jupiter. Don't you read?"

"Yes, I have read *Watchmen.* What do you think I base my life on?"

"Good. That's something we have in common, then."

"Well, what about you? Other than slaying girls in your sleeper van, what do you do?"

"I'm, well…" She trailed off and looked out the window. If there was any sadness in her face, I didn't see it, but there was nonetheless an attractive sense of melancholy about her at that moment. "I'm looking for my father."

"Where are you from?"

"Here, initially, but my mother moved us to BC. With a deadbeat druggie boyfriend."

"I know the type," I said, looking at her as I ordered another coffee and whisky.

"My father tried. He really did; he would always send me letters when he could. But he was troubled—he had mental problems, you know? So I didn't know much about his whereabouts except he was last here. Just outside of Edmonton, that is, at Alberta Hospital. When I went there, they said he disappeared after having a day pass. They didn't put up much of a hunt for him. Gave up after only three days. The thing is, he had troubles like this before and your father Joe had shown him kindness when no one else would. Took him in. You know, gave him food even though your father had none to give. The message I got was only of the highest gratitude for Joe. Said that the sun had only shone on him once in his life."

"That's not the man I knew."

"Yeah, I gathered that from your speech."

I looked down into my drink and finished it, thinking about how you may only know a small piece of the people you're supposed to know best. Our food arrived. Separating my chopsticks then rubbing them against each other to clear off the splinters, I inquired further: "So you thought your old man would be at the funeral?"

"Yes. That's why I went."

We watched each other while eating in silence. She had to be the most attractive girl I seen in a while, though she seemed to go to great lengths to hide it.

"Listen: I know a great bar, and I know for a fact that tonight is not going to be a night worth missing. You game to come?"

"Where is this place?"

"It's called The Bronx. Just across the river. You should come."

"Maybe."

"Come on. Come tonight, and then I want to help you. We'll find your old man and see what this hype is about mine. I don't have anything going on at the moment."

"What, couch surfing, drugs, women, and your so-called revolution gives you free time?"

"As a matter of fact, it does. Kind of depressing in a way; you live the wildest life and all you have is time."

"Okay, come out to my van. Are you done eating?

Man, you eat so slow."

"Hey, Silk, you were the one that raved about this place. I figured I would savour it." I put some money on the table.

The conversation had softened the roughness that I'd been feeling since the run-in with the guitarist. I slid into the passenger seat. The van had a lot of space, red velvet seats, and a good deal of fake oak detailing. The van started with a bit of a fight, and Silk peeled out of the parking lot.

"Hey, now, I'm not used to being kidnapped. I have to get ready for tonight and meet up with some buddies."

"I know. I just want to smoke a bit, and this place would be a little heat."

"Good point." It seemed that her whole life was compressed in the back of her van. A hookah pipe was built into the table, which made me smile.

CHAPTER 26

We didn't talk much as we drove to her favourite spot. I looked at her, but she kept her eyes on the road. There was a strange feeling of understanding, although I still felt a little bit on edge. When we arrived, she turned off the van and made a gesture for me to sit in the back, which I did. I thought of how many people had lived their lives in the back of this van. Even before she had acquired it, it had seen many music festivals and doe-eyed gypsies dropping acid and having orgies. She packed some double-apple shisha into the hookah and added a bit of the weed as well.

"This is the finest stuff you'll ever smoke."

"I have smoked some pretty fine stuff," I said, thinking about how my substance consumption was a bit above average today. I lit a cigarette as she lit the coal and sat close beside me.

"So, you're looking for your old man, eh?" I said, not knowing what else to talk about.

"Yes, and you're going to help me find him, right?"

"That's the plan, yes but I might interject that I'm kind of in a slice of trouble, so I may have to hide out in your van for a while."

"What!? What if I wanted to bring a girl back here? Come on!"

"Those are the costs."

"I guess that'll have to work." She smiled and took the first long drag. I watched the smoke float away, thinking that there had been more smoke in my lungs that day than air. I took the hookah hose from her and took a long hit, seeing right away what she was saying about the bud.

"Where did you get this from?" I asked.

"I know a grower."

"Hmm. Life as a farmer, I've been thinking of giving that a go. Start a small farm somewhere, grow plants and shit."

"Yeah? Plants and shit, eh? You're quite the thinker."

"Some things I give a lot of thought to."

"Like life, I take it?" she said back.

"Well, on this particular day, life is all I've been thinking about."

"Because of the funeral?"

"That, and there have been a lot of new developments in the way things are. Maybe even the way things are meant to be. I've started noticing the difference between the slivers of people that you see and the slivers—sometimes the much larger slivers— that you don't. The things I've learned from you and other people about my father Joe may have just changed my understanding of the man, which I thought would never happen."

"From what I know he was a great guy," she said.

"Yeah, slivers and shadows are all you get from

people; you never get the full story."

"Well, what's your full story? If you were to wear your mind on your sleeve."

"Me? Well, fuck, there's nothing to me. I'm good with girls. I'm nothing, really. Nothing."

"Yeah," she sighed, "I'm nothing as well."

"And maybe that's all you can really be." I sat there with the pipe in my mouth.

The hookah lasted for a while longer and then I sat back down in the passenger seat. The Silk Spectre took me back up the winding roads that lead up the river valley and into the downtown area. A city full of people hiding from the truth that they are nothing. As she dropped me off, I told her if she was going to come to The Bronx to park far away, and even gave her a second location to meet me if the time ran long or if things got carried away. Strange how a day can unfold; the people you encounter. I didn't even know her name, but she was going to be my girl.

CHAPTER 27

I was a little more stoned than I had been all day. *I'm going to marry that girl*, I thought. Back on my bike, the sun was finally starting to dip I kicked the bike into high gear and headed back to the loft—and to whatever fate would find me. I stopped in a liquor store and picked up some whisky and a six-pack of beer. I then continued towards the loft just past the coffee house where I had gained the name 'hun' what seemed like days ago. The Silk Spectre was on my mind. All that mattered was that girl.

I rode up the lift to the loft, finding Matt in the same place I had left him several hours ago.

"Hey, man." I was greeted by the alcohol being taken out of my hands.

"How was today? You guys party hard?"

"Yeah, you know it. What about you? Find that girl? Get her number?"

"Yeah, man. Got her number," I said.

"Decent, man. Ha. It's just me here, now. Mike is going to pick up some entertainment for the night. You got cash? The Bronx is going to be living tonight."

"Yeah, I got cash. Will these drinks cover me?"

"They might, man. Take a seat, I'll get some glasses."

"Hey, bro, you know how much I hate dirtying your dishes. Out of the bottle is fine."

"Alright, sweet."

We both lit up a cigarette and passed the bottle back and forth for a while.

"I saw the guitarist today," I said as I finished a long swig, putting the smoke back in my mouth.

"How's he doing? Playing tonight, right? Opening?"

"Yeah, man, I'm thinking I'm going to rip on stage with him... He's slipping man, you know?"

"Oh, ha. Living the dream, he is. Just like our old mans, eh?"

"Not really. I mean yes, just like our fathers, but he's getting too hard into that arm candy. He's going to fuck everything up—all he's got going for him. It just sucks."

"Come on, man. You know that stuff is the shit. How do you think I spent my day? Course, I smoke it. Needles freak me out. Just the other day you were ripping the pipe with me."

"I know, I know. It's just that shitty switch to the needle."

"I hear that. Quit while you're ahead. Don't want to end up quite like our fathers."

"Yeah, agreed. The guitarist, he's walking down that path and loving it."

He looked at me sideways. "You feeling okay?"

"Yeah, I'm fine. It's just been a shit-show day."

"Whatever happened last night? Did you figure it all out?"

I told him what I knew about the night before: about my uncle's place, about me drugging myself—the whole story—but leaving out the part about giving the homeless man the money and my old man's funeral. Why kill the evening so soon?

"Shit, that sounds like a rager. Sorry I wasn't with you, man. Wasn't my crowd at that show, you know?"

"Yeah, too many 'heads. I was out of my element a bit, and I'm never out of my element."

"Bro, you are a freaking chameleon!" he said, laughing.

"I know, eh? Fuck."

"Well, tonight should be a good time. I feel like I haven't been proper wasted in days," Matt said. We worked our way through more than half the bottle of whisky. When Mike arrived, he was laughing and gave me a hug.

"You kids," he said sitting down.

I filled him in on what I'd figured out about the night before.

"Wild, man. Wild. Well, I've got a few things that might add to or take off that edge."

He pulled out three bags from his pocket: one was weed, one was obviously coke, and the other was filled with pills.

"Whoa. Did you get paid, or what?" I asked, looking at what must have been three hundred dollars or so worth of drugs.

"I had to call in a few favours. What should we start with, boys?"

"I'll take a line of that," Matt said.

"Yeah, what the hell. Could always add a little edge," I said back to Mike as he opened the bag. I rolled up a twenty took back one of the lines. Even the saints are allowed a few sins.

"Good god, nothing but the best for me today," I said as I sat back in my chair. "Man, I tell you: between my uncle's mystery tea and this girl I met from BC, this day has been prime."

"Yeah, man, I bought all this off a biker. He said he had to make a lot of cash fast. Ha ha. Hey, does your uncle still have all that fake money? Been meaning to ask you about that. Could have a little fun with it."

"Really? Not sure about that, man." I thought back on my visit to the farm earlier, holding back a grin. "But this biker. What did he look like?" Mike roughly described him to me and, sure enough, it was the guy from the pool hall.

"Fuck."

"What, man?"

"Oh, nothing. Thought I might have gotten some goods off him early in the week at a premium," I lied. They didn't need to know too much. The coke got me thinking about the shooting, the hit, and the two dead men my father pulled the joke with. My mind started working on the connections. Things were starting to fall together. With the connections, though, came a good deal of paranoia like a bad trip, like the corners of the room darkened. It was something I had to silence.

We sat and drank and I did one more line. I was

pacing myself since I'd already spent most of the day in a blur. I needed a small part of my head on my shoulders if I was going to pull off my joke. Lighting a smoke, I distanced myself a little from the conversation. I could hear the hum of my mind. The kind of thing that meditation brings about; the hum of everything. I put my hands behind my head and just watched my good friends, the lines of life starting to get blurry. The smoke in my mouth went out. I was going to marry Silk Spectre; of that I was sure. I'd help her find her dad, hide out from the 'heads and the bikers, and smoke hookah all day. Lounge away like the Cheshire cat. Life was perfect. Life was the way I wanted it to be. Just making it, barely surviving. That was how humans were meant to live. On the skin of their teeth, with a drink in one hand and a spear in the other for hunting woolly mammoths. I ashed my smoke and joined back in the conversation and, placing my hand on the thick fake roll of bills in my jacket pocket.

CHAPTER 28

We hung out in the apartment telling old stories while getting ready for the night. I sat back for most of this; I had Silk Spectre on my mind and couldn't wait to see her at The Bronx. This meant blowing off both the artist and Rebecca, but if the place got as heated as I expected that wouldn't be a problem.

"You guys getting ready and rowdy?" I asked the guys. "The show will be on at midnight. We should get there soon."

"Yeah, bro. You sure you don't want one of these pills? They'll take you to another level," Mike said as he snorted. My jaw was already chattering a little, so I declined. Throwing on our leather jackets, I took what was left of the bottle and put it into a borrowed military ration flask. We all lit smokes as we entered the lift.

"I'm so pumped," Matt said.

"Yeah, bro, she is going to be a good'er," Mike added as he threw back a pill with a swig from the flask. Pre-game anticipation filled the air as we tried to stand still. Nights with these guys always ended with girls, a fight, or both. I went for the girls, but would never turn down a good fight. The lift took us to the bottom floor, where the sun was finally giving up. We yelled at cars, intimidated anyone that still was slumming along

campus, catcalled girls, laughed, and drank as we
walked.

We jumped the fence to walk across the top of the
High Level Bridge. It could have ended our night if cops
were waiting on the other side like there often were,
but we felt invincible as we stood for a while dead
centre on the top of the highest bridge in Edmonton,
arms around each other's shoulders, staring out into
the dimming sky on the longest day of summer. We lit
more smokes and threw our butts down at the cars that
travelled beneath us. As I looked out, my father came to
mind: the man who was buried that same day. That
even with his drug addiction and hate for the world, he
had left something for me. The man I was sure never
loved me left me the gift of freedom: to come and go
and come and go for the rest of my life. All I needed to
do was to find the last man of that old crew. The one
who was still alive. Searching for people and hiding out
in a van: that was to be my new way of life, and that
made me happy. I felt almost high just off the thoughts.

We started singing underground Irish punk rock—
good rough music—as we carried on across the top of
the bridge. Once we reached the other side, we finished
off the beer and tossed the cans aside. Mike did a few
keys of coke and offered it out; I declined as the
anticipation of the night ahead was giving me enough of
a buzz. Edmonton's downtown died off at that time of
night. It completely emptied except for a few spots with
clusters of bars. The Bronx, though, stood alone as the
home of the punk scene. A type of nursing ground for

my kind of people. There were other places as well, but nothing compared to the energy that the bar gave off. The whole bar breathed, and the walls swelled with smoke and life. We walked down past the Legislature Grounds and, upon seeing some juice monkey and his girl in high stilettos, Mike couldn't resist an opportunity.

"Hey man, better wrap up tonight. She looks like she's been around the block," he said, and we all laughed.

"Fuck you, buddy." The guy stood up. He was taller and stockier than us. He walked towards us and put his face in Mike's.

"Hey, man, you should just take her home and serve her some of those weights you seem to be eating," Matt put in.

"Hey, punk bitches! Run along."

"Fuck you," I spoke as I lit a smoke.

"Let's just leave," the girl said as she came to his side. She looked like everything I resented in a girl.

"Yeah, you're right," he said as they turned—but then turned back quickly and swung his fist and hit Mike directly in the face, knocking him back into Matt's arms. We all laughed as Mike gathered himself.

"Hits just like a girl. In fact, I bet that damsel could give me a harder hit," he said as he spat out some blood from a cut lip.

"What, you want another one, you prick?"

Psycho Mike pulled out his knife. "How about I just split you open?"

I put my hand on his shoulder, "Hey, man, no

worries. Just a small juice monkey. Let's go," I said, calming him down. The guy slowly backed away with his girl, and we were back en route.

All the dogs were out to play. We walked, flipping off cars and drinking some more. Matt and Mike said the pills had started to kick in and they were laughing and running their hands along the walls. I finished what was left of my whisky as we rounded the corner on 101st and there she stood in all her glory: The Bronx.

CHAPTER 29

The buildings loomed overhead of us in this proud, young city. We walked like gladiators who owned the Colosseum and stood with smiles on our faces, joking about our run-in with the couple and wishing we had just a bit more to drink. We flowed up through the line, paid the small cover charge, and got our wrists stamped. I had about three still not completely faded away from other bars and other shows. Heading into the basement to have a few beers, we lit smokes in unison; this was our moment. This was what the previous night—and the whole following day—was leading up to. I got a round for the guys and flirted with the bartender; I knew her well. Beers in hand, we sat close to a table of 'heads I had never seen before. I could just hear what they were talking about over the heavy music.

"They're bringing the money with them, right?" one of them asked.

"They better have that *fuck*ing money, man. Will rest of the guys will be here soon?"

"And if they don't have it?"

"We brought knives for a reason. If they don't have the money, this place is going to explode."

"How many are coming?"

"There's two of them and twelve of us." He leaned inward and I arched back a little, straining to listen. My hearing was surprisingly good, all things considered.

"And did the bikers find out about the cash box? What we need is their lead on that piece of action. That's what they really owe us."

"All I know is that all the men who knew about it, who pulled that job twenty years ago, are all dead. One of them must have given up the location. Those bikers can apply a lot of pressure."

"But if they're all dead, the bikers might not know *shit*. If that's the case, it's lost forever."

I leant back and finished my beer. Matt and Mike were off talking and hitting on girls. So other people knew of the cash box—one of my dad's old crew must have let it slip. If three were dead, my father's suicide must have been a cover. *Damn it!* I cursed to myself. The police wouldn't look too hard into an old druggie offing himself. *The man was killed,* I decided. I lit a smoke. *But who was the fourth member?* The money I took the previous night didn't mean anything: the information was more valuable. I thought through my plan again, feeling the fake money through my jacket pocket. Was my uncle okay? As I ashed my smoke, the red-headed artist spotted me. I looked away and half-hoped she wouldn't see me, but she did and sat down.

"I knew you'd come," she said.

"Hey, baby. I wouldn't miss it. Want a drink?"

"No thanks. I'm already too high for that stuff."

"Might help take that edge off, eh?"

"Naw, I'm good! I'm good. So, are we going to finish our conversation from earlier? How you chewed me out on my life? Because I've thought of a few comebacks to set you straight." Her jaw chattered away.

"And here I thought you would be in the bathroom waiting for me again. Kind of a surprise," I said.

"Not this time. You screwed me over once. I won't let that happen again." She leant forward to whisper. "No, this time I'm holding your hand all the way." She winked and rubbed her nose. "You want a little something?"

"And lose my wits to you? That's okay, I think I'm good." I smiled as I put another smoke in my mouth, which she took and put in hers.

"Come on, now. Let's make this into a real

memory," she said and smoked the cigarette like a pro. Just then, Mike sat down with another beer for me.

"So, who's your friend?" Mike asked.

"Oh, this is the artist from earlier today." They shook hands.

"Girl, you like to party?"

"Hell yes! This prude? Doesn't seem to want to."

"This guy? Really? He wrote the book on partying hard." Mike smiled and looked at me, "Oh, say it isn't true, man."

"Yeah, bro, it is. But don't let me hold you two back. Give'r for me."

"If you insist," she said, taking his hand. I watched them go and drank down Mike's beer. *Well,* I thought, *that's one girl dodged.*

CHAPTER 30

Feeling a little bit tipsy, I headed outside. I noticed Mike and the artist sitting in a car across the street doing lines, but thought little of it. The band rolled up and started to unload their equipment; the guitarist was among them.

"Hey, man," I said. When I approached, he stared at me with a look I couldn't place.

"Ah, hey. Listen. I've been given it a lot of thought—the whole becoming like our fathers thing,"

"Hey, sorry to put that all on you today," I said. He took me off to the side and lit a smoke.

"No, man. It had to be said. I was so wrapped up in this style. I never understood the joke—the joke you laid out in front of me, man. I've lost focus because of my success in this city. Chasing edges, you know?"

"Yeah, listen. It's your life. I shouldn't have said anything."

"No, but you did, though. You're the first to do that. Everyone wants to party the hardest. You used to live or die by that credo, and seeing that you've changed that… You're turning your life around. It's like you see above that line, now. I mean, that's inspirational, man."

He stood there, looking at me and smoking. A kind

of understanding flowed between the two of us.

"Man, I will never touch the needle again. I won't spend my life chasing that dragon. C'mon, fuck that, eh?" He gave me hug. I could tell it wouldn't be as easy as that for him, but his words still made me proud.

"I'm going to get up on stage with you tonight."

"That would be sweet. There are a lot of 'heads here, eh? Fingering in on the scene, the bastards."

"I have a feeling they're here for another reason."

"What do you mean? About last night?"

"Yeah, man. I've got to make a play; I've got to get out of this city tonight. I've met the best random girl. You'd like her."

"Run away as the sun rises, with a sexy babe. That's always been your style."

"Yeah, man. "

"Well, look me up when the heat dies down. What have you got planned?" he asked.

"Ah, you know. Something to piss off the 'heads and bikers, the usual. Except the stakes are a little higher this time."

He nodded, "Hey, listen: I've got to set up. We go on in 45 minutes." He turned, picked up his gear and headed off towards his band. I stood on the corner looking down at the ground; the pavement swirled and flowed.

I walked back inside the bar, back into the basement, and back to ordering beer. I wanted to get closer to that group of 'heads again, but thought better of it. All I had to do was find the fourth man in the cash box scheme. Then I'd take off to the country, raise chickens and goats, grow my hair long, and wear a large white woven poncho. The notion made me smile, but I had to keep an eye on the crowd. I didn't know when the other players from earlier that day or even last night would recognize me. I faced the bar, wondering how I could steer Rebecca away when she arrived. How I could deflect her? I was just hoping she was drinking. It made her a bit more chill when she was. I ordered a shot of Jack, then waited.

CHAPTER 31

The show was going to start in a few moments when I saw Rebecca.

"Can I buy you a drink?" I said casually.

"Do you have my money?" she countered, raising a cynical eyebrow.

"Your money, eh? Is that all you care about? I thought me and you had a thing going this morning. Some good sexual tension."

"You dick. Just pay up. I know you've been on the hustle all day—the lengths you're going to. It's sad, man."

"Two bottles, please," I said, raising my fingers to the bartender who nodded her head.

"Alright, Rebecca. Let's see, now… How much do I owe you?"

"It's not just the money I want."

"Sexual favour?"

"Stop." She smiled. I smiled back, lighting a smoke and sipping my beer. "You know, there's something wrong with this scene. Don't you feel it?"

"Not sure I understand."

"I've been thinking today about all the drugs and hate that run through this 'revolution.' You must feel that, right? That hate?"

"The hate is new, but it'll get pushed out. This is still the only way to live," I said back. "What? I know when you get your degree you're just going to jump ship. Find a nice guy, maybe. Someone who plays sports, not an instrument."

"I'm just tired of all the lying. Of all the untrustworthiness. I mean, I liked you at one point. I liked you a lot. But then when you ran out on those drugs and left me with the bill, I wanted you dead. That anger scared me. I thought that wasn't what the scene was about."

"You would rather peace and love, like the hippies?"

"Sometimes. I mean with each generation the

drugs just get harder. The lifestyle gets harder. The hippies had it right; there were no lies. No cheating."

"That's quite the insight just from me running out on a tab."

"You just don't get it. The way life just dies off. The 'heads? The bikers? What part of the scene do they fill? Pushing drugs and causing fights?"

"And what part do you fill?" I asked.

"Me? That's the point. I don't fill any part. I'm quitting. I think you should too before you die and leave nothing but people pissed off at you. Just get out."

Her eyes were hiding tears. I thought she must have been on something—or maybe she'd just had a day like me. I faced the bar and ordered another beer. She told me not to worry about the money and slid away into the crowd. With a beer and smoke in hand, I thought about her words. Before today I would have never left the scene—never given up on the 'revolution.' But now it seemed it was more important for me to piss people off and get messed up. I was starting to fight more, and that was not the revolution I had in mind. Maybe the hippies did it best with their brown bags, soft drugs, and good-time vibes. I felt the fake money in my pocket, nicely-coloured paper. really. Did I have to start this fight? What was I becoming? Maybe this would be my final joke—my send-off. I'd look for the fourth man, help find the Silk Spectre's father, and then get out. Drift the trains to Arizona, get the cash box, then start a farm. The idea was becoming increasingly appealing.

I lit another smoke, hoping my pack would last the rest of the night. Then, I found the clove cigarettes in my other pocket and a small sense of relief came over me. I thought back to our conversation and it seemed that Rebecca must have been waiting to say that to me for a while. I put my beer down and headed back out into the main bar. The show was about to start, the band performing their sound checks.

Silk Spectre was still nowhere to be seen.

The crowd—my fellow revolutionaries and I— stood near the front. I noticed the bikers and the 'heads standing at the back arguing with each other. They must have been speaking about the shot deal, and it looked heated. The band took to the stage. The guitarist saw me and gave a small gesture. The rest of the band had beers close by, but the guitarist didn't. They finished their sound check as I looked over at the 'heads who were scanning the crowd. I hunched forward at the front by the stage, wondering what they'd found out. The band started to play, and soon it was time for me to make my move. The money would hopefully launch a brawl and take the pressure off me, then I could get out. The music started, the words resonating. I started headbanging and a circle began to form near the stage as fists and elbows were thrown. The 'heads stood close on the other side of the pit. When the first song ended, the band waved for me to get on stage with them.

CHAPTER 32

There was no hiding now. The guitarist gave me a quick nod and I glanced back into the crowd, looking at all the 'heads, the bikers, and the rest of the community. I jammed along with the band and, out of the corner of my eye, I saw people advance as they recognized me. Silent figures moved through the roar of the crowd. Everyone from the night before was there. I could see the 'heads standing on the other side of the pit and, beside them, the bikers from the pool hall with harsh bandages on their injuries. All of them just watching. This, my last performance, my last hurrah before the end of the world, boiled down to this moment. I reached into my pocket as the song reached a peak and pulled out the cash. I could see that the crowd paid little attention to me. But the 'heads had noticed me—and so did the bikers. One of them raised a baton and pointed it at me while another a 'head flashed a gun. I held the money and sang as they kept pushing through the crowd. I held up the money, took the elastic off the roll, and threw it into the crowd. The men advancing stopped as they realized what was happening. Soon, everyone rushed the mosh pit and a fight broke out as people scrambled over the money. Jumping off the stage, I ran for the exit. The 'heads paid me no mind as they started brawling with the bikers; the tensions between the two had finally erupted. Bouncers rushed in trying to break up the storm that I started. The band's next heavy song flowed along with the chaos around as if it was all part of their show.

The door opened, and I was out into the night. I ran, partly wishing I had another long line in me. I raced towards the bike, then heard a shot ring out. Hot behind me was the old biker, broken out from the brawl. The man could move; he was on my heels and firing shots. I kicked the bike off as I dodged the gunfire. He started after me on his own bike, weaving through traffic. My adrenaline was running high. I would have to lose him before meeting with Silk. He followed me down the hill into the valley, where I took a sharp turn onto a bridge around a blind corner. Thinking fast, I slammed on my brakes. The biker tried to do the same, but couldn't. He slid off his bike, skimming along the ground like a rock on water. As he slid to a stop, his bike slammed into the bridge railings. I stopped and ran towards him.

"I'll fucking hunt you! I'll never stop! You're a dead man. We will find you and kill your *fucking* family. You're dead!" He shouted at me, but he was in too much pain to pick up the gun that was only a few feet from him. "I'm going to fucking kill you!"

I didn't think twice about picking up the gun and turning it on him.

I rode away. It was time to hide out. The 'heads and bikers would be too busy killing each other, but my chance wouldn't last. I went too far back there and had only doubled the pressure on my head. Riding past our second meeting place, I caught sight of the Silk Spectre's van idling. Still in a panic, I ditched my bike and left it to slide down towards the river. I dusted off my jacket and pulled out a very bent cigarette, lit it, and rushed over towards the van.

CHAPTER 33

"What the fuck happened?" she shouted as I got in through the back.

"Silk! Chill. Everything is okay," I said, panting, sitting myself in the back of her van and fumbling with my smoke. "We need to go to my uncle's farm for the night and lay low, though. Okay?"

"I saw you on stage. What was with all that cash? Was that the biker's money? Did you steal it? Holy shit, what a show! I've never seen such a scramble. And that biker who followed you out—did you lose him? What should I be terrified about first?"

"Don't worry about anything. Just drive; I'll show you the way. Calm down and just get us to Sherwood Park Freeway,"

"I'm calm. I'm calm. Man, oh man. You're crazy. The police started rolling up as I was leaving that fucking place."

I sat in the back, blowing smoke out slowly, trying to control my breathing, thinking about how well it had all gone. I wasn't going to dwell on the biker; the slate would soon be clear. I was leaving the scene—leaving Edmonton. All that mattered was the promise I had made to this woman about finding her father. "Listen. Once we find your dad, we've got to leave for a while. You know of any place we could go?"

"Yeah, I know of a small cabin in BC that's pretty far out of the way... Do you have the cash to get us there?"

"No, but I think maybe I can get some from my uncle." I couldn't slow my heart down as I moved up to the front seat.

"Fucking first dates, eh?" Silk sighed.

"Reckless life, right?"

"Yeah, reckless life."

I sat low in the chair and chain-smoked, shaking my head.

"How did you like the show?" I asked as we continued through Sherwood Park and out towards country.

"It was pretty good. There's a good scene here in Edmonton. I had no idea. But you guys seem to really like your drugs."

"Yeah, everyone there was strung out. Putting edges on."

"And you? Do you have an edge on? You must." I remembered the joint Mike had slipped me for setting him up with that girl and pulled it out of my back pocket to light it up. It felt no different than tobacco at this point.

"A little at the beginning of the night, but not too much. The drug scene is almost as big as the music. People get into it for the music, but the drugs follow shortly after. Soon, it becomes less about the music and more about chasing that edge, you know? What's the scene like in BC?"

"It's different. A lot of hippies, a lot of... I don't know, wasted life. It's all just wasted life."

"And what would be a better way to live? To be consumed with your job and making money? Everyone has a fixation in their life. Everyone has one thing that they put above the rest. Every life has some centre. Music and drugs, that's just *our* fixation."

"But how long can something like that last? Eventually, you'll burn out or die. If you burn out, it's like you have to start your life back at the beginning. You have to give up the things that gave you life. But then all you do is just replace those things with something else."

"Yeah, just start another fiction. There is no true road."

"Even after tonight, you'd say that? Never change,

never think you'll lie in the gutter, look up, and find God?"

"She is in the sunrise. We'll see her today, I expect. I don't think sleep is on the agenda."

"God is in people..." she said. I looked over at her, almost stunned by the expression. I appraised her, her eyes focused on the road and the street signs. There was God right next to me—the girl I would marry.

"That's what I've always thought."

She looked over at me for a moment. I lit another smoke and turned on the radio. The top story of the hour was a small riot that had taken place in the downtown core; a punk show that got out of hand. We looked at each other, then back at the road.

On my signal, she turned onto a dirt range road which we followed to my uncle's farm. The lights turned on as we drove up. He came out onto the front porch, poorly concealing a shotgun in his coat, but a broad smile cracked across his face when I stuck my head out of the window. Laughing, he came to greet us.

"Still alive, I see."

CHAPTER 34

"I've been listening to the police chatter. Did *you* start that mess downtown?" My uncle had something resembling true concern on his face.

"I may have had a hand in it. Can we hide out here until morning?"

"Sure. I've got a few beers—and a few other things that might tickle your fancy," my uncle replied.

"Let's start with beer."

"And who's your friend?" he asked as the Silk Spectre got out of the vehicle.

"My name's Ellie." *Ellie,* I thought. Somehow that name sounded familiar. But from where? I was happy calling her the Silk Spectre, but where had I heard the name Ellie before?

"Is that your name, now? I thought I'd never learn it." I smiled as we walked to the porch. Sitting down, my uncle opened a cooler filled with beer.

"So, you two meet at the show?"

"No, actually, she knew my old man. We met at the funeral today."

"Well, I didn't know him personally. Joe knew my father—who I'm looking for—and he would always speak highly of the guy. I thought he might have been there."

"Spoke highly of him, eh? Must have been the only one," my uncle put in. We cracked a couple of beers and we all lit cigarettes, watching the fireflies and the other bugs fly around. Nobody said much as we sat. I started to think about how good to me my uncle was; how he would always take me in after a night of partying. The man was like a father. I drank my beer, my hands still shaking, while Ellie and my uncle talked. I admired her, seeing God in conversation. I was thinking back to waking up in that ditch, caught up again in the circle of thoughts I had carried throughout the day. It occurred to me that's all someone is: their circle of thoughts. There's a universe of ideas to think about and learn, yet we are all trapped in our habitual thinking. That's how you know you're beginning to die: one day your thoughts don't change. I thought of the look on the old biker's face as he held his legs in pain.

"And then he scattered the money into the air," Ellie finished, as I tuned in.

"What? Really?"

"It was fake money, Uncle."

"Wait? Fake money like that old 'paper' in my barn? You managed to start a riot with that shit money?"

"Yeah. Don't worry, though. The 'heads and bikers are going to be at each other's throats for a while."

"So what happened to the real money?"

"Well, you know me and material possessions."

"Yeah, I know your stoner-brain personality. What

did you do with it?"

As I stared off into the horizon, the name finally hit me. Ellie was also the name of the homeless man's daughter. My heart lifted. If that was her father, then he must have been the fourth person involved in the cash box heist; the details surely fit. I stood up out of my chair and laughed.

"Hey," my uncle reacted, "what's so funny?"

I turned and faced the two of them. "I gave it all away to a homeless man. The man said he was going to put it in his daughter's bank account—his daughter named Ellie." Everyone stood up with a start.

"Are you saying you met my father? Did you give *him* all the money? Was it really him?" she asked, staring at me.

"There's a good chance." I grabbed her hand. "And there's a good chance. I think I know where to find him!"

She hugged me, "Oh man, that's awesome!" She held on for a few moments before separating to walk off the porch and gaze out at the stars.

"Uncle, there's a good chance that her father was the fourth man in the cash box scheme."

My uncle leant forward. "Are you serious?" he asked.

"Yes. If he's where I think he'll be tomorrow, we'll find out. And Ellie and I are the sole inheritors of the cash box."

My uncle smiled and sat back in his chair. "I never thought you would find that man and so quickly. You bastard, I always knew you were lucky. In one day you start a war between those filthy heads and bikers with one hand, and with the other you find the only man alive who knows where the cash box is."

"If he is where I think he'll be. We'll know tomorrow just after sunrise." My uncle smiled as he sparked a joint up and passed it over to me. I took a deep drag and lounged back. "There's a small problem, though: tonight. the bikers were going to give the 'heads the cash I stole and information on the cash box. It seems one of the four men let something slip. Three of them, including my father, I think, were killed in that process."

"Killed? How much information did they give up?"

"I don't know. I doubt very much. If any of them were like Joe, they would have given up very little. But still, tomorrow we're going to set off for Arizona with Ellie's father." I gestured toward Ellie, who was just out of earshot. "Would you want to come?"

"That's okay, couldn't leave my cows."

"Well, I'll keep you posted as to things go. I haven't told Ellie yet... Look are her, man. She's beautiful." We both gazed at her as she danced on the lawn looking up at the stars, lost in her own little moment.

"So, who killed your father? And the other two."

"Some fucking biker, I don't think he'll be after us anymore."

"What makes you think that?"

"I just wouldn't worry."

He took the joint from my hands and ashed it on

the tray. We both sat and watched Ellie.

"You know, I'm going to marry this girl."

"Something's with you. Something's changed; you're just not the same. What's up? Yesterday, all you would have talked about was womanizing. Now you say you've found the girl for you?"

"Just had one of those days, you know? Saw the sun through the sand storm." My uncle looked away. His face squinted as if my words stabbed at him. My heart was pounding. *I'm in control,* I thought. *I'm in control.*

CHAPTER 35

I walked away from the porch and set out to see the cows. Thoughts were running through my head of how all things come together. Of how life begins to make sense in a way. All the chaos and disorder evenly dissipate. I walked into the fields as I smoked. The lights from the porch were getting further and further away and all that remained was starlight; the 'heavens.' Earlier that day I would have told off anyone that said so, but it was as if the skies had opened up. I thought of how people feel that God has a plan for them. This seemed to be true, but maybe people only thought this way when everything fell together, and when things fall apart they pray for the day it will all come back.

I could hear the cows off in the distance. I had made up my mind that when I found that cash box I would start a farm. A farm far away—away from my crew and away from the scene. A sign of rebellion against rebellion. The ultimate way of going against the new. Farmers may, after all, know what's best. The cities infringed on them, and they said 'No.' They said: 'You cannot. You must stop. You want my land? You'll have to take the deed from my dead hands, as I will never become one of you. I will never live between concrete walls with all the noise and the cars and the hate and the misunderstandings.' Life is on the farms. It all starts in the bush. 'My house is on a dirt road that winds and bends and is unmaintained, so you have to have a 4x4 if you want even a small chance of visiting me.'

That's how life should be, I decided, and for a moment I saw myself on my own porch with a cigarette dangling from my mouth and refreshing lemonade perched beside me. The Silk Spectre and I would watch the road, but no one would come because no one would know where to find us. Life would be complete. The scene and the revolution that I once held so dear would go on without me, and other womanizers and others testing the waters of drugs would fill my place.

I looked back at the porch. Ellie was back sitting with my uncle—the man who understood the way things were. Like my father, the man who just yesterday I would have spit on the ground over, but who in the end had this grand plan for me. The way he treated me had me convinced I was nothing to him, but maybe Joe knew that all it would take was a day like today to get me to change from his path. I would laugh and raise a glass in his name. It wasn't just about him hiding away the money, though. Maybe he was just waiting for me to come into my own. Maybe that's why he never hunted me down after I stole his bike. He knew that the bike would force me to feel the air on my face. The bike would force me to feel. I had never made my peace with him, but one day I would.

One day, old friend, we will understand each other, I thought as I looked up at the sky.

I started to walk back across the field towards the porch. The silence of the farm was all-encompassing. I would need a gun from my uncle; it might be a rough dash to the border. Would the Silk Spectre's van make it to Arizona? I sure hoped it would. I walked back to the porch as the two of them rolled another joint, looking out at the sky that was so dark but yet already held a little slice of dawn. A little hope.

"Just in time, eh?" I said grabbing another cold beer.

"Yeah, I was just telling Ellie here about the tea we had this afternoon."

"It sounds very compelling," Ellie said.

"Yeah. Eye-opening."

"Well then, it's decided," my uncle said. "I'll put on the kettle." He walked towards the burner. "A little weaker than before; don't want you two love birds up all night."

I looked over at Ellie, who smiled at me as she smoked a cigarette. The girl from BC looking for her father: the man with the keys to our future There wasn't a doubt in my mind that we would find him in the morning on the same bench, with the same smile.

CHAPTER 36

I finished my tea and stared out at my surroundings. The starlit sky, the company, and the whole day had changed me. I was put back in the spot where I was just after the funeral. The ideas the tea brought were just as clear. The world, my life, the lines, and the way people live in it—everything was clear, but it held this new nagging fear on reality I couldn't place.

"So, you two are to be rich and happy. The good life," my uncle said with his eyes closed.

Ellie swayed her head and looked at me. I felt the clarity in her soul, in her eyes. Running my hand through my hair, I let out a long gasp of air, feeling my lungs empty and then refill.

"Yes, we are. Together—we're going to start a farm." I searched Ellie's face for a hint of resistance, but she just smiled. Maybe it was the tea, but her expression suggested it was her idea all along.

I turned back to my uncle. "I'm a little worried about the gangs. About how much information they gathered, and whether or not they'll try and run us off."

"I have just the thing for those bastards. Just give me a minute." My uncle slowly rose from his chair and walked inside his house.

"Rich and lifted of the curse of life, eh?" I said to Ellie, still thinking of her as Silk Spectre in my head.

"The curse of life?" she asked. I felt her words float across me. It seemed that her hair was lifting and flowing around her head and it was hard to find the words that I needed to say. I shut my eyes. It broke the illusion, but with my eyes closed I could compose myself.

"The curse of life." I repeated. "The systems in place that everyone fights for: the money, the no money, the love, the no love. The be-all-end-all. The material, the fixed, and the empty spiral. Together we will rally. Together with the spirit of the land. We will have a farm and trade with goods and services. We'll live in peace, ride horses, and master many musical instruments. Like free people. We'll eat fresh fruit off the trees. Animals will roam wild on our lands, and we will know them as our gods and treat them as such. And in that way, the curse will be lifted. We will return to the way of Adam and Eve in the garden—the 20th-century version. The money that is in the cash box will grant us this life as if it is not money, but an elixir of life." As I said the words, I recognized they were just the ramblings of my high state. But I felt as if the theme was to be true.

She looked at me. "I will say nothing."

My uncle returned and stretched out his hand revealing a Colt pistol. "You may be needing this."

I stared at the gun. It grew and warped. The drugs still ran my mind. My uncle led us off his porch and over towards some hay bales. Placing bottles and directing a spotlight on them, he laughed, "Time to learn how to shoot. Your old man really should have been the one to teach you, but I'll have to do."

Ellie was slowly dancing beside me, and I woke from a layer in the dream world. I focused, fired at the targets, and the bottles shattered. My uncle gave me tips after I fired each shot. I was sobering up a bit from the tea; my vision was starting to come back to me. Ellie was still lost in a haze.

After three rounds, I was doing pretty well. My uncle laughed. The tea had little effect on him since he drank it so often. At the end of the shooting session, I didn't know how much time had passed, but I felt good.

We headed back to the porch.

"That was just what I needed. Feeling that old happiness again," the Silk Spectre said.

"Puts a smile on your face, eh?" said my uncle.

"It definitely does," she said, licking a rolling paper.

"I have a spare room for each of you."

"I'll sleep in the van, if that's alright with you," I put to Ellie as the romance of the drugs—and the state of peace they brought about—wore off. Still, I thought that Ellie and I had a future. But as with any drug, you aren't the same afterward. Part of you changes, maybe forever, and the thin grip you hold on the world is loosened.

"Sounds good," she said and passed me the keys. I tucked the gun into my belt as we smoked the joint. We didn't know the time. During high summer in this part of the world, the sun rises early and never really sets. I could just see the beginnings of dawn.

When we stood up, Ellie headed towards the house and my uncle followed me part-way to the van. "I'll wake you two up in a few hours with coffee." I nodded to him, knowing that Ellie's father would be waiting for us. I passed out as soon as I closed my eyes.

CHAPTER 37

My nose started to itch before I was fully awake. I didn't know what day it was, or where I was, but I knew that smell: the kind of smell that wakes you up early on your days off.

I felt a sharp push on my shoulder and opened my eyes to see my uncle across from me with a coffee in a tin cup.

"Here," he said, passing me the cup.

"Thanks, man," I said, taking in my surroundings. Sitting up, I drank all of the warm black coffee in one go and sparked a smoke. Soon, the Silk Spectre opened the door and joined us in the dimly-lit van. A wave of light followed her.

"Ready?" she asked.

"Yeah. You're driving, though. You know, I don't know what it's like to wake up anymore. I don't know what it's usually supposed to feel like."

"That's good," my uncle said. "Means you haven't had a dull night in a long time." He stood up in the van as Ellie got around him and started it up.

"I guess this is goodbye to you two. I assume you're going straight after the cash box?"

Calmly I nodded as I extinguished my smoke and

smoothly lit another. My uncle leaned over and shook my hand.

"You may not have done the old man proud, but you have by me," he said.

Not knowing how to respond, I just thanked him. Noticing the gun on the table, I quickly hid it away under a seat, wondering how much use it would be out in the 'Wild American West.' Jumping into the passenger seat with Ellie at my side, we left on the dirt road back towards the city.

"Are you excited to meet your old man?" I said just as we turned off the range road and onto the highway.

"I've been dreaming about this day for a long time. All I have of him are his letters. To meet him in the flesh will be like meeting someone who was lost their whole life. To meet the man, finally, face to face, will be incredible."

"You shouldn't... I mean, shouldn't set your expectations too high. He is just a man—a confused person, you know? What's your plan once we find him?"

"It's like you said: he can come with us and guide us to the cash box. Do you think your Adam and Eve story has room for one more?"

"Oh." I looked away, embarrassed. "I was hoping you wouldn't remember the high ramblings of last night. I was not my usual charming self."

"I didn't mind. It was sweet—kind of sweet. You've got a bit of a hippie child in you. It's starting to come to light. Maybe the drinker and the womanizer are all just a shell hiding the soft heart of a flower power child."

"Hey, now. That's not me. I'm as hard on the edge as it comes, just was high! It meant nothing. The curse of life—I remember saying all that stuff. But the edge is on and it will always be on," I said and sparked another smoke, my armour back in place.

"I'm just kidding. Hey, if you want to be the first punk rocker who turns hippie—trades in his coke for acid, his prescription pills for homegrown weed, and starts listening to Janis Joplin—that's your demon to deal with."

"Shut up! Ha. I will always be punk rock. Having a farm and a horse will just make me all the more feared."

"Is that what you're really after? Fear?"

"Fear and power."

"Ah…" She looked at me, smiling. "You're so full of shit, you know that?"

I flicked the smoke out of the window. "The fullest."

We drove towards the bench I had visited the morning before, and there he was. It was the same man as before, but he wasn't sitting. He paced—looked agitated and troubled. He wasn't the calm man I had talked about our broken society with. Something wasn't right. We found a place to park. I looked anxiously over to Ellie, but her eyes beamed with excitement.

"Alright, let's go!" she said opening her door, but I grabbed her arm before she could step out of the van.

"Wait! Something's not quite right. He doesn't

seem the same as before."

"Come on man, let me go. I have to see him. He's my father; I'm sure he'll know it's me."

"Okay. Be chill, though," I warned as she hopped out the door. I slowly got out, watching her skip over to the man. I threw my smoke to the ground and followed.

CHAPTER 38

Ellie stood by her dad as he paced.

"It's all a joke. It all has to do with God, the world, the last supper—the joke's on them. I'm not going to listen. I'm the second coming: part machine and part man. I'm the second coming of God. They're waiting for me. Always waiting. He spoke to me. Some might think it was ringing in their ears, but it was the angels telling me that I was the white horse. Musicians know they have always been trading skills with the devil."

"Father, stop. It's me. It's Ellie. Stop and look at me!"

"I have no daughter. Light brought me into this world. I read the signs, the patterns, the cars, the

shapes. Artists harness the devil: it has all been said."
The man was pacing around talking quickly, walking in
one direction then stopping and turning as if held up by
invisible forces.

I didn't know what to say. It was the same man I
had met the day before, but something was missing in
his eyes. Was he that high? An unfortunate mix of hard
drugs? I stood by Ellie as she pleaded with him.

"Father, look at me. I've travelled here to find you.
Please, sit down. Let's talk. Remember the letters you
wrote?"

"I cannot write—I can only see. The only things I
could put on paper were propositioned by the devil."

"No. Father, the letters you wrote me and I wrote
you—do you not remember?"

"They are waiting for me to bring down the church.
That is my mission. They are all led by the devils and
their politics. And the prostitutes. And the filth. And the
drugs. War is to be waged, and I'm the one to bring it to
the church. I know the secrets. I know all that they tell.
The message that all women understand. I love them to
death, and they hate me for it. The ultimate end. The
way an artist dies when he pours himself into his work
with his muse burning his soul white. No one is real.
Everything is a copy. Come with me, and I will show you
how to kill yourself—how to be free. Nothing matters
on the other side. With me all art is easy. Everything
makes sense if you only see the message for what it is—
see the world through the right lens."

"Listen, man, what have you been taking? You

were fine yesterday. What happened?" I asked him. I spoke calmly, but he looked right at me—or more through me—his eyes wide and dry as if he hadn't blinked all night.

"You. You were the one with the money. Can't give it back to you. Put it in my daughter's account. Same numbers. I deposited the right sequence of numbers, so that she would get the message. Spent a little on myself—to take the edge off, you know, then everything made sense. Couldn't go on resisting temptation, you know. Had to taste the water one more time."

"Hey, buddy, this is your daughter. She's standing right here." Ellie was close to tears as she reached out to touch his shoulder.

"Can't be. She told me she was dead, but I know she isn't. I know she is the fourth disciple in my coming—my rising. I will die and rise again."

I was looking over at Ellie, not knowing what to do. I lit a smoke and offered one to him, but he just stared at it. I raised my hand with the pack, a single cigarette protruding.

He took the cigarette, smoked two puffs, and then in a fit, tore it to pieces.

"The devil's magic! How dare you tempt me with the church's control tactics?"

"Hey, man. Sorry. I thought it might calm you down. Have a seat."

"Sitting is for the weak. I will never sit, nor sleep, nor love, nor dance."

"Father, please." Ellie reached out to him. "Please sit." He looked at her in a daze, as if he hadn't seen her until that moment, and sat down.

We sat on either side of him.

"You have to understand, both of you, that I'm not of this earth. They are always watching. They are watching us right now. You must understand!" He grabbed my shoulders and shook me. "You must understand."

"Man, I do, but this is your daughter. We're here to help you. We're here to get you off the shit heap. Come with us." I put my hand on his shoulder as he broke into sobs; I hadn't seen a man cry this hard in my entire life.

"Give me one of those smokes," he said without looking up.

I looked over at Ellie, who looked terrified. The man sat back up, tears streaming down his face, smoking rapidly.

"Who's watching you, Dad?"

"Everyone. The church, the police—they have spies in every corner of the world. They were waiting for me to come back, see, they're trying to snuff me out. Don't you see?" He gestured his head to some people that were just going about their morning business. "They are all spies, every one of them. Not to mention the satellites that trace your every move. They hold all the keys. They will kill you with a laser beam that shoots down your head and melts your spine."

"Hey man, we aren't in on it. Come out into the open world. Your daughter has a van where you'll be safe."

"And how can I trust that you're not just another spy?"

"You know me, man. And you know your daughter, Ellie. We found each other in a mutual search for you."

"No one has ever looked for or cared for me but one man: Joe."

"I'm his son. I will show you the same kindness that he did."

"Ha ha!" The man went from crying to laughing in an instant. "The stuff me and him pulled, that old bastard. I think I'll look him up." I made eyes with Ellie, shaking my head. "Alright, if you're his son and you are in fact my daughter, then I must go with you. You two will help me bring down the church. Yes, I can sense it. You are the first of my disciples. Yes, it is true: in the night God came to me and told me I would find you two in the morning. I remember now."

We stood up together and headed towards the van, walking slowly as his head was swaying and his attention snapped from the trees to the parked cars and up towards the sky. It was as if his mind had no inner guide. We passed a man in a suit.

"The message, sir! Learn to understand the message!" he shouted at the man, who was startled and quickly rushed away.

We got him to the van and opened the back door. He started laughing. As we got him inside and closed the doors behind him, Ellie and I stared at each other, speaking in whispers.

"We have to get him help," I said to her.

"No! We can help him. He'll calm down. He must have been mixed up in some drugs last night."

"No drug cocktail on this planet would do that to a man. He's mentally ill."

"Great thinkers usually are," Ellie said back to me.

"Ellie! I'm all about fucking the rules, but this is too fucked. He'll bring too much attention on us. Try to understand that we can't take him across the border. And we have to go—people are hunting me." We could hear loud banging inside the van. "Ellie, we'll get the money in Arizona together, but we have to take him to the hospital."

"All you care about is the cash box. This is my father! He stays with us."

"Come on, Ellie, he doesn't even know who you are."

"Listen, I still don't even know your name, and I took you in."

"What the fuck! You didn't take me in."

"Whatever, punk."

"No, listen to me!" I grabbed her. "This is not your father; this is a shadow of the man he is. Let's get him help. We'll put him up in the hospital where they will help him. They have drugs that will calm him down—get him thinking straight. We can put him in for a while, then come back to sort it out. But I have to leave town, and I need you to come with me. We need that money he was talking about in your account. Come on, Ellie."

She looked away from me towards the van. The

banging around had stopped.

"You have to promise me we *will* come back for him."

"Yes, I promise. We'll get him help, get the cash box, and he'll be better when we get back."

"Promise."

"Yes, I fucking promise! Let's get out of here." We stood for a moment in front of the van's back door, hesitating before we entered.

CHAPTER 39

As we entered the van, Ellie's father was holding the gun.

"Hey, man. Put it down," I said, as Ellie gasped.

"Such a funny thing—such power that one can hold. With a tool like this, people listen to you. People fear you with a thing like this."

"We *are* listening to you, but we're *not* going to fear you. You're a smart man, just going through a rough time—standing on the edge of oblivion like the rest of us. All you have to do is look down and say 'Not on this day. Not today.' Come on, put the gun down."

He looked up at me, his eyes starting to water. He put the gun on the table, then I took it and hid it from sight.

"Not on this day," I repeated.

I was more worried that he was going to kill himself; I didn't think he could harm us. Manic or not, he still had a moral compass.

"I'll drive," I said to Ellie, who sat in the back with her father. I slowly took the van towards the closest hospital, not knowing what outcome lay ahead. I drove almost in slow motion as if I was on a drug myself. The smoke from my cigarette left my lungs and held in the air briefly before the breeze swept it out of the slightly-open window. The speed of life: slowly exhaled, then swept away in a quick rush. The rush was the part we were all in now. I didn't think Ellie's father would tell us where in Arizona the money was in the state he was in. Not a chance. The secret would be lost forever. Maybe the money I had stolen from the bikers would actually be in Ellie's bank account, and it might get us far enough. I did still have to leave the city, and quickly.

I pulled into the university hospital, wondering how to make the next play. The van gave a jerk as it stopped and I looked in the side view mirror, considering the man's dark paranoia. Was he right? No, he couldn't be. Slowly switching the engine off, I stood up and joined the two in the back, sat down, then lit a smoke.

"Just five more minutes, okay?" Ellie said to me.

"I know where you have taken me. This is the den of the church. Do you know what they will do to me here? They will empty my mind of thought, and I will become a walking void. Oh, it has happened before. I won't be able to hear the birds. I won't be able to walk hand in hand with my creator. I will become empty—that is what they will do to me. It is the cycle of my life."

"Listen, man, you may get all those things, but they will make you better. They may numb you for a while, but it will get better. You will be able to recognize faces, and you will be a step closer to your maker. He has shown you the world in ways people will never know, but you will heal. Never forget this day or the days in the past. I promise you, when they release you, your daughter and I will be standing there waiting with open arms. And then we will all hide away. Together."

The man had settled down. His eyes were still racing, but there was some calm there. He nodded his head.

"Don't you see? You must see, you are my disciples. The last supper, the world, the whole prank. Pulled quite a prank in my day."

"We know. There will be time for more talk—more redemption—but this has to be dealt with first."

Together we exited the van and slowly walked up to the emergency ward. Ellie's father had his head down as if he was willingly embracing defeat—or more likely, he knew he could have won but had been given orders to lie down and surrender anyways. We all sat down in the emergency. The man starting sobbing again. I sat on one side of him, Ellie on the other, in the dull green waiting room. Other patients looked over at us, holding their elbows or holding back coughs. After a long hour, the nurse saw him. Ellie gave him a hug. He stood up, lifted his head, and was willingly taken away. Nothing said.

Ellie and I left the hospital, being told that he would be admitted for thirty days. They would contact us after his assessment. We sat in the back of the van and I held Ellie's hand as she started to cry. My uncle had slipped a cigarette carton into our pack, so in an attempt to comfort her, I lit us up two smokes. Only then did I notice something out of place on the floor: In a pile of assorted maps, one, weathered and almost falling apart, bore a title that read, 'Welcome to Arizona.' I spread it open, then stood up with amazement; sure enough, the location was marked.

CHAPTER 40

We left the hospital. Would he see his treatment through? I slowly rounded a corner, wondering if it was all real: the day before and the moments of this morning.

"How did he know?" I gestured with the map to Ellie, speaking through an exhale of smoke. We headed to the South Side of town where her bank was.

"I don't know. Hey, do you think we did the right the thing?"

"Silk, he needs help, and we got it for him. When he's better, we'll all meet up again. The heat will have died off and we can go anywhere as a team. We did the right thing."

"I need some weed."

"Of course. I can hardly put up with the boredom of driving as is and we have to go roughly a day and a half straight."

"I don't know, I had only seen him as a young kid and that meeting may have been my only chance to see him again. What if he disappears? The money doesn't really matter to me. He does. He helped me understand the world when I was younger, you know?"

"You will see him again. We have a month for our adventure. A clean adventure, which I haven't had too many of. Come on. Things are on the up, Ellie. Let's get good and stoned and just drive."

"Yeah, just drive. That sounds good. I didn't sleep last night, so I might just pass out and take the night shift. How far do you think we'll get today?"

"Pretty far. I think we'll at least get across the border before it's dark."

We drove to her bank. I puffed away in the van as

Ellie went inside. I felt the pulse of my body, the excitement moving through me. My senses were overloading in my state of idleness. In the side mirror, I saw some bikers turn into the parking lot. The guys looked at little too familiar. I headed to the back and, with the shades drawn, I took out the gun as they parked beside us. My ears rang with the intensity of my heart beat.

"Let the 'heads handle it, man."

"That bastard's as good as dead. Everyone is looking for him. He shot our guy in cold blood."

"We have to watch out for the 'heads too, man. They're after our gang. We have to lay low. They want that money too much to let that guy get away."

"How did the 'heads get so big anyways? Since when did they rival us?"

"Lots of hate these days."

They were walking away from the van and into a small corner store. I didn't think anyone saw the van last night. I thought back to my bike, which was probably unrecoverable now. I'd miss it, but the van was surely safer.

I saw Ellie leaving the bank, carrying a thick envelope. She saw the bikers and approached them, and I dropped my smoke in shock. *What the fuck is she doing?* I swore silently. *Does she want to have a tea party?* I anxiously peered through a small crack in the shutters. Then I rolled my eyes as I saw she was buying weed from them. They casually finished the exchange, then Ellie returned to the van and climbed into the driver's seat.

She was laughing as we were pulling out of the parking lot. "Nothing like flirting with danger, eh?"

"You are one crazy broad. You know that, Silk?"

"Hey, reckless life. Let's switch seats and I'll do some rolling."

"Alright." At a red light, we both jumped out and I got back into the driver's seat, slamming the door shut just in time to make the light and make our start out of the city on Highway 2.

CHAPTER 41

"Ellie, before you pass out completely..."

"Yeah?"

"Why does anyone worth their salt get baked all the time? I mean why give up every drug but not weed?"

She smiled and laughed. "We smoke weed all the time to slow the pace. To relax. I've already kind of dealt with full speed enough this morning, haven't you?"

"Yeah. It's just—I mean the lines. The lines of life: maybe they are meant to be seen."

"What are you even...? Look. Life is crazy. The world is crazy. Don't you think Gaia put a little something on this planet to blur existence?"

"But you know when you see a truck commercial, and you see the one guy doing a chin-up and another guy closing the button on his suit, all after they get out of their loaded pick-up truck?"

"Where are you going with this?"

"I don't know, just... What I'm trying to say is, do we really know how to act? Is the imagined way of how things are supposed to be just lived out in commercials on TV, where everyone is perfect? Is that what we are after? I mean, is that what we are all striving towards?"

"Of course, we are. Don't you want to be in a gun fight and not be hit? Find love easy? Have pretend hardships, and then get taken to a castle where everything is all good?" She laughed again.

"I may be high, but that doesn't seem very good to me. Not like a reckless life."

"But even that's flawed, don't you think? Don't you think living the life of rebellion is just another made-up story?"

"You know, I've been thinking that way all day."

"There is no way to really be free from cliché."

"I know, but there must be something you can do."

"I don't know man. Want me to roll another one?"

"You know it, babe." As she busted up the weed, I gave her a smoke to add to it; we needed to stretch it out.

"What are you going to do with your share of the money? Go into the wild and pick berries?" she asked.

"Nah. Hopefully, I won't go on too big of a bender. I want to enjoy it for the rest of my life. I told you about the farm, right?"

"Oh yes, the farm. I can't believe you want to just leave the punk rock scene without a fight and become a dirt jockey."

"I'll build an empire of dirt."

"You know, when I first met you, I didn't think much of you. I just assumed you were wasting space, and that you didn't want to help me find my father until you found out about the cash box."

"Hey… that's not true."

"You strike me as the type—well, the kind I don't usually mess around with."

"This may be the weed talking," I said, noticing then that I was driving well under the speed limit. "But those days are behind me; the difference a day can make."

"Dinah Washington."

"You know your music."

"You know, punk, you may just have a chance with me on that farm."

"I would like that, Ellie."

"But man, I'm tired. I need to stop thinking for a while. Wake me up when we reach the border or when you get tired of driving." She passed me the joint to finish. High thoughts aren't clear thoughts. In the absence is when you truly think. The weed did practically nothing, but it helped me remember the high of the tea.

We had travelled past Calgary, but I decided to go more eastward on odd roads. Smoking slowly, I found an old tape of CCR songs and sat as low in the chair as possible. What had happened to me? I was not the same as before. Maybe I was having a mental breakdown myself, but how could you tell? *People don't just change,* I thought; no one I knew had ever changed. The world just gets harder, life grinds along, and you never really grow up, and things just eat at you until you become bitter. In the kind of place where you find yourself asking, 'Why?' Until one day you just stop and accept it all. People just want to become more comfortable. 'Leave me my chair and my TV. Take my freedom, but leave me my chair and my stool to put my feet up. I've worked all day. I've done my part, so just leave me my chair.'

Soon we would have the cash box. Soon, the dreams would all come alive and all the moments of clarity would come to pass. Throwing the rest of the joint out the window, I felt happy with my thoughts. Didn't even really care if I was getting us lost. It was in this moment that I noticed that a rusty old red truck with two men sporting shaved heads had been following us since we passed a small town named Duchess or something. Looking at the gas meter, I noted that we had about a quarter of a tank. I cut down a gravel road after seeing an old beat-down sign that read

"Dinosaur Provincial Park." The quick turn woke Ellie up, and we started heading into a small patch of desert in southern Alberta.

CHAPTER 42

"Ellie. Take the wheel, eh?"

"Are those 'heads? Fuck. How long have they been following us?"

"I'm not too sure, but we're going to have to deal with them."

"What does that mean?"

"Listen, take the wheel and find us a quiet place to pull over. Away from civilization. I'll hide in your storage closet, okay? Talk to them, but don't mention me. Word must have spread about what happened in Edmonton. Just act natural; it'll be fine."

"Okay, punk... If you say so." She moved across the middle of the van and we awkwardly changed places. I moved into the back, lighting a smoke before putting it out again immediately, realizing I couldn't smoke it in the closet. I was still feeling pretty high, but I was a good shot in spite of the tea the night before. I Picked up the gun, threw the clothes out of the closet and hunched down inside. Closing the door gave a firm click; too firm. I could feel the van slowly roll to a stop and then heard the truck behind us stop as well.

"Hey, what do you assholes want? Why are you following me?"

"Shut up, bitch. You're on the wrong road with too much bad luck. You get around in this rolling sex house, don't you? Get out here. Now." I could hear the door forcefully open. Now was my chance—fucking 'heads. I would sneak around back and scare them off. I tried to crawl out as I heard Ellie scream, but the closet door wouldn't open. *Fuck. Fuck,* I thought, pushing on the door. I couldn't understand what they were saying until Ellie shouted.

"Get your hands off me! I haven't seen that mother fucker." Ellie was shouting frantically.

"Come on, you BC whore. Get on that hood."

Still, she didn't call out for me. The door wouldn't open, so I started throwing my shoulder into it. Still, it wouldn't budge. *Who installed this fucking 'roided-out door?* I didn't know what to do. Those assholes were going to rape her. I couldn't let that happen. I could hear more shouting. I leant back in the cramped closet as far as I could and threw my shoulder at the door with every inch of my being. The latch broke. Kicking open the back door, I saw the two 'heads trying to tear Ellie's jeans off. They stopped in bewilderment, gaping at me.

"Mother *fuck*—" the first 'head started, then I shot him twice in the chest. The other guy ran to the door of the truck and pulling out a shotgun. There was ringing in my ears from the two shots I fired. I had no thoughts. Just action. I fired first; another splitting bang rang out in the desert as he fell back, firing the shotgun wide. Both men were dead. Ellie ran to the front of the van as I climbed into the back, and she peeled out so fast I could barely close the door.

"You asshole! How could you let it get that far? Mother *fucker*."

"The door stuck! You should have mentioned that it's a fucking lead-lined bomb-shelter closet. Who even put that in?" We were driving quickly out of the park and back towards the highway.

"Why the fuck would I know!? You dumb mother fucker."

"Listen! Chill. Nothing happened. We're in the clear."

"It's what could have happened, punk." She shook her head, yet her eyes held no tears, and surprisingly she wasn't shaking. She must have been in that kind of situation before.

"Fuck, *fuck*," she said again.

"What!?"

"You just killed those assholes!" I hadn't even thought about it. The night before came to mind. The biker who chased me from The Bronx. Had I now killed three people? *It was for survival,* I told myself. *It was them or us. I had no choice.*

"You'd better get rid of that gun. Let's stop in the next town, grab a bite to eat, and get rid of that goddamn thing."

Before we entered the small town of Lethbridge, I cleaned the gun and threw it in a gutter. It left me feeling relieved and human again. Then we quickly carried on and stopped in a small diner's parking lot just outside of the city. Ellie said we could afford to eat better then fast food, and I agreed. Before we went in, we sat, lighting a joint in the back of the van.

"Never," she said.

"What?" I said back. "Never what?"

"Till the end of our days, punk, we will never speak of what happened out there."

I took a drag. "Deal."

"Promise."

"Yes, I promise."

"Good. Now let's leave the reality behind, get high, and drink coffee."

"Promise?" I said.

"Shut up." She smiled, looking away. We walked into the diner, both wearing sunglasses, took our coffee black and then started eating large amounts of pie, pancakes, bacon, and sausages swimming in maple syrup. After we were good and sated, Ellie said she was good to drive for a while and we started to make our way to the border.

CHAPTER 43

I was staring out into the great unknown, mentally sifting through our situation. A long road lay in front of us. The road less travelled; our path to freedom. One does not often think about thoughts, step out and just analyze the chaos. To be on a real train of thought is a rare occurrence. You can find peace in your mind. Day in and day out you think the same things: I should buy this, I should buy that, I should drink less. It's all the same, but then there are those days... Maybe the sun is hitting your face in just the right way. You've had just the ideal amount of caffeine. Then, for once, your mind honestly thinks. Riding in the passenger seat of the van, I was having one of those moments with a cigarette hanging from my mouth, not noticing the ashes falling onto my shirt. I had just killed. I had just taken lives. I was doing the world a justice; I had put an end to evil. But then there was the path those two 'heads will never get to walk. Maybe before all the hate filled their lives they would fish together as the sun rose, little kids with sticks and worms for bait. Maybe it was the polluted air that filled their hearts with hate for other cultures. Whatever the fact, they were not always that way and maybe they could have changed. That was something else that bothered me, but I didn't want to let that take over my thoughts at the moment. The fact remained that they were going to do terrible things to Ellie and kill me for the cash box. Evil men, in the moment. Why should I hesitate?

There was a small line of vehicles crossing the border. I rolled down my window and took a swig of some water, cringing as if all liquids held the flavour of alcohol.

"What should we tell them?" Ellie started.

"It's simple. We say we are going to Arizona to collect millions of dollars that were stolen from a drug deal fifteen years ago. Simple." Ellie gave me a blank stare as I coolly smoked another cigarette and smiled.

"We're doing this, then?"

"Of course. We are mere days away from the revolution of our lives. The kind of thing that doesn't happen; the kind of revolution that that will bring about the downfall of the civilized world."

"Oh yeah, I see you have big plans. Going to sell beef jerky on your ranch and win the hearts of the people."

"Exactly."

The line of cars moved along slowly.

"You think my father will be alright?"

"Yeah, he'll be fine."

"Are you sure?"

"A few years back, I had a friend who thought that aliens were reading his mind and he would wear tin foil hats to stop them, as cliché as that is. Kind of your typical breakdown, I guess."

"Did he get help?"

"He did."

"And?"

"Well, he's sane now."

"But not happy? Not better? Not the man he used to be?"

"Well, no. But sane."

"What a thing to happen. To lose your mind, and then all you want is to be back in that high because life is so blah afterwards," Ellie said.

"And, of course, the very things you use to escape from that fact are the triggers that start the breakdowns again. Life has some very dark irony."

We approached the crossing booth. "Can I see your driver's licenses, please?" the official said.

We both handed them to him. "What's your business in the United States?"

"Getting hitched in Las Vegas. The drive is part of the pre-honeymoon," Ellie told him.

"Are you, now? Well then, have a safe trip." He tipped his hat with indifference and, just like that, we entered Montana. The air seemed to change as we entered a new country. The land of the free: a term used loosely, I thought, but used loosely by so many.

"That was the truth, wasn't it? That's what you really want? For real?" I asked, throwing my cigarette out the window. She looked at me and gave me a smile: the smile I was starting to get familiar with.

"Of course."

Part of me, maybe the part that was still a kid,

rejoiced. And for the first time in long while, an honest smile crept across my face.

The sun passed. Ellie and I had switched driving. My hope was that we could make it to Vegas by the next morning, sleeping in shifts. Thinking back to the fake money in The Bronx, the riot that started because of it, the tea with my uncle—that damn tea changed so much. All these thoughts seemed to be part of a separate life. Another person. A different person. I was a new guy. That damn tea. And here was Ellie doing all this travelling with a man she was planning on marrying. Whose name she didn't even know.

CHAPTER 44

Everything is interconnected through the web of the universe. All of us are under the same sheet, and here I was tearing holes. But then again, someone had to; someone had to say, 'fuck the white sheet.' It was one thing to join others in the act. But to be truly free was to have no one—no way of life. To be a part of nothing. Was that the path of a true artist? Maybe it was, but it sure seemed like the right path for me. And that was what I was going to do on my farm. At the end of my gravel road, I would sip my coffee as the sun rose and wear the same patched jacket and pants till the sun set again. Have some old truck that I would learn to fix, have a lot of books, and just read all day with Ellie. We would be happy knowing that we were both part of nothing and both the centre of the world at the same time. The centre of the fabric of which everything was connected; the pin that held it down and stopped it from floating away. I chain-smoked. I couldn't stop my mind. It was as if these thoughts belonged there. I had always known what I needed to do. Known what being a part of the community was leading me to. All those good times that I wasted having good times, as the Animals song goes.

Looking out my window, I saw more of the grid I wanted to go off of. I had never been to the States before. The way my father would speak of them left little desire in my mind to get out and explore. Now, I thought how this place would be my new home. This was where I was to build my tower, in the old Wild West.

"We should make it to Vegas by morning, if we don't make too many more stops," Ellie said.

"Yeah, that was my thinking as well. You think we'll be able to get hitched first thing?"

"Oh, most definitely. That's still the plan."

"You're not getting cold feet, are you, Ellie?"

"No, not me. One life to live, right? And a reckless one at that."

"Exactly. Let's get some road drinks in the next town. I'm getting shaky."

"Good call. Some liquid lubricant will do me well on the night before such an important day."

"You weren't a little girl dreaming of a big dress, were you?"

"No, not me. That wasn't really in my thoughts. I've been playing the part of a lesbian for quite a while. Well, sort of."

"Seriously? When I first met you, I thought you were kidding."

"Nope. It was more to stand out, really. I *am* bi, but never actually went for guys. You know, just a way of pissing my mom off."

"For how long?" I asked.

"Well, up until the time I met you." I looked over at her. She had a serious look on her face. My jaw dropped a little more than I should have allowed.

"I knew I was good with girls, but I never thought I was *that* good."

"Hey, punk, don't flatter yourself," she said looking at me, "I was just waiting. Laying low. But when I met you, I knew."

"You say it so matter-of-fact."

"Yeah, well, life is pretty matter-of-fact. If you wait, you keep asking yourself why bother, right? Might as well just go into things head first without hesitation.

That's the only way, you know?"

    I looked forward, smirking a little. She couldn't be more right. Getting married wasn't really on my list, but fuck it, why not? The sun was setting as we stopped to eat. I had to try the fast food this time. Some places in the world have monuments, others have art and history. America, in my mind, has fast food. After we had eaten, my whole body felt like it had aged a few years. We also picked up some American cigarettes and alcohol. I sipped beers while Ellie sipped tequila, but she assured me she was going to pace herself and not pass out before our big wedding. The lights on the van were as crappy as anything, but I wasn't bothered. The road wore on with us laughing and joking. She was the one for me; she was to become my wife as the sun rose in Vegas.

CHAPTER 45

"If you can dream and not make dreams your master..."

"What was that, Silk?"

"Oh, just a part of an old poem," she smiled.

"If you can think and not make thoughts your aim," I said back to her.

"Wow, you know it?"

"'Course, I know it. Rudyard Kipling. It's famous."

"'If,' what a poem. My father, he wrote out that poem to me in one of his letters.

"And you being a girl didn't factor in?"

"Hey, asshole, it doesn't matter who you are or where you're from: that poem rings true at any point in your life. Old or young, male or female, or whatever."

"Yeah, my father had it engraved on a cigarette holder that I would steal smokes from."

"I can't believe you know that poem. Doesn't it just give you the shivers? Doesn't it awaken your soul?" We were both feeling pretty tipsy.

"Yeah. I used to think I had everything in that poem figured out. I used to think I of myself as the son he was talking about, you know?"

"Then what happened?" she asked.

"I grew up and realized that I was none of those

things. I realized that the world, and everything in it, was not mine and I was no man. Then I just started to say, 'screw everything,' you know?"

"Yeah, the first time I read it, 'to hear the truth you spoken twisted by knaves to make traps for fools...' That was my father. That was him; he was speaking the truth, and it was getting twisted. That rang true with me. And also, the idea of thinking and not making thinking or dreams your aim. That was me. I was just a kid in a dream world. How did that poet have it all figured out in the 1900s?"

I grinned.

"You know, we are becoming those men. This trip, this journey, getting married—we are that 'man' he speaks of in his poem. The world is ours, because we have courage."

"You're totally right, Silk. It's the background to our story. Walk with kings—nor lose the common touch."

"I'm going to get that tattooed in Vegas," she said.

"Yeah, we should both get the poem tattooed."

"But of different parts."

"And we are becoming men. I hope that was the metaphor and you aren't going to go after some young Vegas girl."

"No, punk, I'm sure about you. This is a great idea! There has got to be some parlour open that early in the morning."

"It's a deal: you get a sparkling unicorn with a stanza below it, and I'll get fire and brimstone."

"We're becoming men, punk. We'll both get fire

and brimstone."

"Agreed."

We drove through the night only encountering a few scattered cars. I was becoming a man. I was becoming the man from that poem. I no longer craved the highs. I was to start a new life. Then it dawned on me: what it meant to start a new life. I couldn't go back to Canada. Surely the 'heads reported back to Edmonton about seeing the van and me, and now everyone was probably on the lookout. At least we made the border, but it seemed to me that my Canadian days were over—at least for a long while. I would have to make a new home in this old country. I would start over. Running from the bikers and the 'heads would be easy here. No one would follow us this far or think that we would hide out in such a place as the Arizona desert.

We smoked American cigarettes as we drank and I thought more of our lives back in Canada. Only then did I remember that we had to go back to get her father. Would Silk be okay with doing it alone, just weeks after our wedding? It would have to be that way. There was no home for me back in Edmonton. I slowly drank another beer, thinking how I could not risk going back across that border. I would have to make her understand. The beer was numbing my already-numb thoughts while I let Ellie drive.

We were deep into the night when, off in the distance of the desert, we could make out a beam of light shooting up into the sky. I hadn't slept. The thought of telling her I couldn't go with her, that she would have to get her father by herself, was stinging in my mind.

Before I knew it, Ellie had driven us into the early-morning traffic and onto the main strip of Vegas. We both put our heads out the window; the sights were incredible. I was struck right away. I had an urge to drink and gamble—and maybe do a mountain of cocaine. We pulled up to the largest hotel we could find, got a room, and I passed out on the bed.

CHAPTER 46

My eyes drifted open. There in front on me in low-cut white dress was Ellie.

"What do you think?" She asked.

"You look gorgeous."

"Thanks. I laid out a suit for you. Kind of guessed your size. Get up and try it on."

I sprang myself to life. Sometimes, only a few hours

of sleep can do a man wonders. I quickly put on the suit and balled up my jacket and clothes.

"How hot is it outside?" I asked.

"Kind of like the surface of the sun."

I smiled at her. I never liked suits because they never fit, but here Ellie had picked out one that fit perfectly. I decided that this was a good a time to style up my Mohawk and then we left the room and went out onto the strip. Ellie wasn't kidding; it was fucking *hot*. Nobody stopped to look at us as if we were an all-too-common sight. We decided to go into a liquor store and buy another small bottle of tequila, pouring it into a flask that Ellie said came with the suit. We took swigs from it and looked around.

"We have to be quick, eh? I want to reach the cash box by at least this evening,"

"Yes, of course. Our adventure. I haven't forgotten."

We hailed a cab and asked him to take us to the roughest 24-hour tattoo around. He laughed, saying there were a few, and soon we were getting our forearms shaved and prepped. We kept drinking from the flask; the artist said it was alright with him if we bled out.

"So, what will you two be having on your big day? Matching hearts with unicorns or something like that?"

"Naw, man." Ellie said, "I want the quote 'If you can bear to hear the truth you've spoken twisted by knaves to make traps for fools, if you can trust yourself when all men doubt you, but make allowances for their doubting too.' That over fire and brimstone would be perfect."

"Awesome, brah. Never heard that line before. Did you make that shit up?"

"Heard it somewhere."

"Cool, cool. I'll get to work." And the artist started writing the quote on Ellie's forearm without giving much thought to how, but it began to look pretty good even though he was pretty much just free-handing it. I double-checked to make sure everything was spelt right, but the man was good. He finished the quote quickly in a flowing cursive and then started adding a fire beneath it. Ellie was happy, and she took the flask from me and smiled. "Your turn."

"And you want the same thing?"

The buzz from the night before had never actually worn off, and a new smooth edge was taking hold. "I want, 'If you can dream and not make dreams your master, if you can think and not make thoughts your aim, if you can meet with triumph and disaster and treat those two imposters just the same.' But with the same fire beneath it."

"That's way cool. Where did you guys hear about this poem? What's the whole thing?" The artist said, pausing with the needle close to my arm.

"Don't know, man. Just some guy who heard it from some old guy."

"Humph." He started carving up my arm. The pain was intense. I didn't know how Ellie handled it so well; even in my state it still hurt like a bitch.

"Keep your secrets then, you two."

I lit up a smoke. I was also bleeding a lot more than Ellie, but the guy didn't mind. Ellie was humming to herself in her white dress which had gotten a bit of blood on it. In about the same amount of time, he had finished mine with the same cursive. I was amazed by the rush it gave me. That was the way to take an edge off. I already wanted another one. Ellie just laughed as she paid the man with cash from her bag. The man waved as we walked out the door. In the sun with the rush of dopamine, I held Ellie close and gently kissed her.

"Better kisser then some girl?"

"That was pretty good. But you still have a few things to learn, punk."

"Ha." I started looking out for a cab, my mind felt clear with this new type of rush. "Man, that's a better high than most drugs."

"I hear that! Give me another one of those smokes."

"Sure," I said. We stood on the sidewalk for a moment to finish the cigarettes, then found ourselves making out in the back of another cab. The driver was barely able to hear our request to go to a church, but he figured it out.

CHAPTER 47

"Hey, cabby. How about a hundred dollars and you be our witness?"

The fellow happily agreed. The church was small, and a janitor was cleaning up what looked like throw-up. We walked up to the front desk were a soft-featured woman greeted us with a brief smile.

"We want to be married as soon as possible, please," Ellie said.

"Alright, you two lovebirds. Welcome to the Church of Elvis. I have a few papers for you to sign and we'll get things underway. Do y'all have a witness? I could do it for you if you'd like."

"That's alright, ma'am. We already have this fine gentleman here for a witness," Ellie put in, playfully.

Our taxi driver stepped forward, taking off his Tigers baseball cap, and signed the document.

"Hey, man. Why don't you be my best man for another hundred."

"Sure, buddy. No problem." The driver grinned at his large, unusual tip.

"Aw, I want a bridesmaid," Ellie complained.

"Well, it's not busy here in the morning, since most people do this when they're all liquored up. I could be your bridesmaid."

"Perfect," Ellie said to the woman, and after the papers were signed the woman presented us with a bottle of cheap complimentary champagne which the four of us took turns drinking as we waited for Elvis. This was the only way I was ever going to get married: with a fresh tattoo and strangers all around. Ellie pulled me by the arm and we stepped outside for a smoke.

"I just realized my father's not here. I always figured if there were one day he would show up, it would be this one."

"Hey, Ellie, it's alright. We'll meet up with him in a month's time. I bet the news will be so shocking to him, we'll have to put him right back in the hospital."

"Shut up. Asshole."

"Sorry, that just came out wrong. Didn't know what I was saying. I just mean the guy will be happy."

"Yeah, you're right. It's not a joke, though. His mental health is not something to be laughed at."

"I know, I'm sorry. Hey, let's just forget about it. In less than ten minutes, our fates will be tied: mine, yours, and your father's."

"Thanks for saying that, punk. You know, I should learn your real name pretty soon, eh? Didn't catch it when you were signing the papers."

"Let's save it for the last minute. You do realize that once you hear it my spell will be broken and I'll just be another guy."

The woman from reception came and grabbed us. She had been chatting with the driver and it turned out they had a lot in common. Tigers fans and such. I walked down the pews and shot the janitor a wink. He shrugged indifferently and raised his broom.

Standing at the end of the aisle, Elvis looked at me and quietly, out of character, said, "Nice suit man."

"Thanks."

Then the music started and Ellie walked down the aisle. When she reached the front of the room, she stood by my side along with our paid witnesses who were both grinning.

Elvis said a few words about rock and roll, then looked at Ellie.

"Do you, Ellie Vauhan, take Raphael Smith to be your husband, in sickness and health?" Ellie stared at me and smiled.

"I do," she said.

Then Elvis looked at me. "And do you, Raphael Smith, take Ellie Vauhan to be your wife, until death do you part?"

I looked at Silk, my chest slowly rising. I paused briefly to bug her. "I do."

"I now pronounce you husband and wife. In the name of rock and roll, you may now kiss the bride."

I grabbed Ellie and held her tight as our mouths locked. Our company gave out a cheer and Elvis made a few more trademarked lines, then we ran out of the church, laughing with each other. The cab driver quickly came from behind and herded us into his cab, then proceeded to drive us back to the hotel.

"Didn't think you had the balls, Mr. Smith," Ellie said.

"Nor I, Miss Vauhan."

We looked at each other, indifferent to our given names. "But the adventure is just beginning, and there is much to do." And without changing, we hopped back into the van. I was driving, so I gave the map a quick skim while I lit a smoke all in one fluid motion.

"Let's roll, sugar," I said, peeling out of the hotel entrance and out onto the road with my new wife, racing out of the town and off to our last destination and to the end of the story. The land was unforgiving as we moved forward. Ellie decided to roll a few joints and we passed them back and forth as the road winded and turned. My thoughts and dreams all seemed to blur around us. The blurred lines, the lived lives, and the unlived. Now all I had to do was be a man and tell my new wife she would have to leave me soon.

CHAPTER 48

The desert grew more enjoyable as we drove through it, even though the heat was intense and the van had little to no air conditioning. Stoned out of my mind, I would frequently check the map: 'Flat-faced boulder, west of centre,' the red hand-written letters directed, pointing near a side-road intersection. We drove on, getting closer and closer to the goal. We spoke little in our high states. Excitement and bewilderment filled the air.

"Is this really happening? Is this story really going to have a happy ending?"

"It is, Ellie."

"Most stories are just let-downs. Life is not the dream you think it will be. There is always something or someone that lets the story down—some event that ends childhood and happiness."

"Like your father's situation?"

"Yeah, that ended the dream for me. His story and the sadness it brought always follows me around. The emptiness: not knowing where he was, not knowing if he was even still alive… That ended the dream for me, especially, when it clicked. You know, when I understood what was going on."

"Me as well. Had to do with my father at least. The dream ended early for me. That man was cruel. I never liked him, and I grew to hate him."

"That's hard. But hey, your father did leave you with the opportunity to go back into the dream world— as did mine. They both had this whole plan for us."

"Bizarre, eh?"

"Are we getting closer?"

"We should be there soon. Man, oh man! I can't believe the course a life can take! The unknown scramble of events. Makes you think there is a plan.

That there's sense in the chaos."

"Are you talking like there is a god?"

"Maybe, yes… But not so much a god as a 'ray of hope' that guides you. If you asked me that a week ago, I would have given you an entirely different answer."

"Maybe you're on to something. Did we just become Christians or something?"

"Nah, more like Buddhist."

"Agreed, Raphael."

"You know I haven't heard my name spoken in a long time. You and Elvis are the first to hear that name since I dropped out of high school. I always had a made-up name for everyone else. If no one knows your name, the name you give them becomes the vessel for who you are."

"You're a strange guy, my husband."

"The world's strange. Life is crazy."

"Yeah. Just the way I like it. Pass me another smoke."

"Sure thing. Hey, listen. I've been thinking… I'm not too sure I should go back to Canada."

"What!? We have to get my father."

"I know. I'm sorry. But as the events unfolded on our drive, I just don't think it's such a good idea. The 'heads know who I am and they will kill now. Like, on sight."

"I can't get him by myself dude, come on." The van started to sputter. "You know how to talk with him."

"Fuck."

"You have to come!"

"No, the van, Ellie. Shit, we are *so close. Fuck.* It's cutting out."

"I can't believe you, Raphael."

"I think this van is more of a pressing matter right now."

"No, it isn't. This isn't over. You have to come with me and take the cash box back to Canada."

I was looking down at the speedometer as the van came to a crawl. The music cut out.

"Ellie. Silk, listen. Take your half with you. You can rent a car, go get your dad, and then we'll meet in the countryside. I'll buy a farm here in the States and wait for you there. It has to be this way." I couldn't focus on the conversation as the van sat dead on the gravel road; we were so close.

"How do I know I will ever find you again? Man, this was what I was talking about with the dream getting screwed. *Fuck.*"

"The dream isn't screwed! Chill."

She kicked the dash in frustration.

"Listen, we have a month before he's out. We'll work fast and get established, then you can go meet him. It has to be this way."

"Okay. Fine. But now what are we going to do? We are completely screwed."

"We'll finish the trip on foot. We're *so close.* Let's focus on finding it. We'll figure something out," I said loosening my bow tie. "It's going to be hot, though. We should strip down."

We both got out of the van and stripped down to

our underwear. Ellie thought ahead and had purchased some strong sunscreen. I applied it with a smoke hanging out of my mouth, grinning at her, trying to soften the tension. We grabbed as much water as we could carry in a small backpack along with a telescopic shovel and a half a six pack, and I wrapped my shirt around my head to protect my partially-bare scalp.

We started off. The land was barren, and we had only moved a little ways before we needed to take a break and drink some water. There wasn't any sign of shade, just some valleys off in the distance. I took note of where the van was as I stood to continue on. My head was clear; the dream was at hand. I reached out and held Ellie's hand. At first, she was a touch reluctant.

"Weren't you saying the other day that you wanted to work on your tan?"

She lightened up a bit as we continued walking, watching small lizards run around. Smoke and determination kept us going. This was to be the day that would change everything. This was to be our finest moment. The sun would not deter us, nor would the world.

CHAPTER 49

"I mean if there is a god, she would be out here. Out on the edge of the world where everything looks bleak and dead, yet there is still life."

"Punk, you just summarized all of life."

"I kind of like the clockmaker theory. That appeals to me: some force crafted our journey and we just walk it. You know, our parents' lives, our lives, everything leads to a point: this point. And even our revolution is just another play acted out."

"There is no way that all thoughts and all love are random. Out of the chaos, there is some order," Ellie said.

"I'm just saying that the chaos may be a type of god. But the order is the mind, the person holding the thoughts."

"So, the mind is man's, but the soul belongs to another 'being.' Really it's just old-school philosophy."

"Yes. The mind dies, but part returns to the chaos. That would be the only way I would be satisfied with the thought of a god, I think." I stopped walking and stood in a small clearing. Ellie almost walked into me.

"Let's have some more water and a smoke." Sitting down, I lit a cigarette. Ellie and I stared at each other with sweat pouring off our brows and down our faces.

"You're the last person I would have figured I'd end my days with, punk."

"Yeah, I know. I kind of hate myself for arriving at such conclusions. It just all came to me these past few days. I was far from being clear of mind, but all the drugs and drink did something to clear my thoughts. It set me free. You'd think all that would be brought by those indulgences would be a complete lack of clarity."

"I see," she said.

"You're not convinced."

"You're my husband now, and I would even follow you back into The Bronx." She smiled at me. "Should we keep moving?"

I stood up, "I don't think we have much farther to go."

"Why's that?"

"Because—" I grabbed her by the shoulder and wheeled her towards what had just caught my eye: a large, flat-faced boulder leaning against a small hill—no more than a football field away.

"Oh my god. We made it!"

I shouted, pulling out the telescopic spade from our pack and racing towards the destined landmark. Ellie trailed close behind with our pack in hand, both of us laughing as we closed the distance.

We reached the boulder in half a minute, stopping at a spot near its sheared face where the wild grass and cacti were especially patchy. I quickly started digging. Ellie cleared away the sand with her hands and feet. I couldn't get the smile off my face.

But after digging and sweating for an hour, I wasn't smiling anymore and was starting to get worried. How deep would they bury it? Was it even here? Did we find the wrong flat-faced boulder? Was any of this real? Finally, my shovel hit something and gave out a loud 'clang.' Praying it wasn't just a rock, I jumped down on my knees and, using my hands, scraped around it. I soon found the corners of a steel box. Ellie joined me and, working together, we exposed the top of a green metal military box. We looked up at each other.

"Is this for real?" she said.

"If it is, then there must be a god, and she is great."

Digging further along the edges, I came across a pair of handles. We both grabbed a side and, with a mighty heave, pulled the cold box up onto the hot sand. I sat back against the large rock panting and, for some reason, I looked around to see if anyone was watching. There was a small lock on the lid which only took four blows with a sharp rock to break.

"Go ahead. Open it," I said, covering my eyes.

With my eyes closed, I could hear the lid open and Ellie scream. I slowly allowed my eyelids to open to see the piles of money: hundred-dollar bills stacked high. I fell to my knees and lifted a stack; there were more beneath it, and more beneath that. Jumping up, I grabbed Ellie and we started dancing around in joy. It was all there. It was true, and the dream was real. Ellie sat back by the box and lifted a small envelope that had fallen to the side.

"When I lifted the lid, this was just laying on top."

"Open it up," I said. It was full of old Polaroid pictures of the four men—the men that pulled off this scheme. Sitting with our backs to the cash box, I cracked open a watery American beer; warm as hell, but the best beer I'd ever had. My old man, the world, the universe—everything had happened for a reason. When all was lost, the man I hated had truly set me free.

###

Acknowledgements

Thank you Alma Visscher for the cover art, edits and love.
Will Gabriel for the final copy editing and suggestions.
Friends and family for the never-ending support.

Punk

Made in the USA
Columbia, SC
12 April 2019